Brock

7 Brides for 7 Blackthornes
Book 5

ROXANNE
ST. CLAIRE

Brock
7 Brides for 7 Blackthornes

Copyright © 2019 South Street Publishing
Print ISBN: 978-1-7339121-3-6

Published in the United States of America

Critical Reviews of
Roxanne St. Claire Novels

"St. Claire, as always, brings a scorching tear-up-the-sheets romance combined with a great story: dealing with real issues starring memorable characters in vivid scenes."
— *Romantic Times Magazine*

"Non-stop action, sweet and sexy romance, lively characters, and a celebration of family and forgiveness."
— *Publishers Weekly*

"Plenty of heat, humor, and heart!"
— *USA Today's Happy Ever After blog*

"It's safe to say I will try any novel with St. Claire's name on it."
— *www.smartbitchestrashybooks.com*

"The writing was perfectly on point as always and the pace of the story was flawless. But be forewarned that you will laugh, cry, and sigh with happiness. I sure did."
— *www.harlequinjunkies.com*

"The Barefoot Bay series is an all-around knockout, soul-satisfying read. Roxanne St. Claire writes with warmth and heart and the community she's built at Barefoot Bay is one I want to visit again and again."
— *Mariah Stewart, New York Times bestselling author*

"This book stayed with me long after I put it down."
— *All About Romance*

7 Brides for 7 Blackthornes

Meet the Blackthorne men, who are as hot, fast, and smooth as the whisky that built the family fortune, and the yachts and race cars that bear their name. From proud Scottish stock, Blackthornes never lose. But, one by one, the seven sexy men in this family are about to risk everything when they fall for strong and beautiful women who test their mettle in life…and love.

1. Devlin by Barbara Freethy

2. Jason by Julia London

3. Ross by Lynn Raye Harris

4. Phillip by Cristin Harber

5. Brock by Roxanne St. Claire

6. Logan by Samantha Chase

7. Trey by Christie Ridgway

For more about all of the 7 Brides series and a complete list of books by Roxanne St. Claire, go to www.roxannestclaire.com.

Brock

Chapter One

The transition from King Harbor to Boston was never nice and easy for Brock Blackthorne, but tonight it felt particularly wrenching. Leaving the family estate on the peaceful, picturesque coast of Maine and making the two-hour drive to the pressure cooker of Blackthorne Enterprises in the heart of the city always felt a little like crashing through a plate-glass window very much like the one behind him. Although, as always, the shades that covered the commanding view of Boston were closed tight, making sure Brock didn't catch even a glimpse of the skyline or harbor, a nausea-inducing fifty-three stories below.

In Maine, where he'd spent most of the past month, Brock always felt the tension ease from his shoulders and any anxiety melt from his chest. A razor rarely touched his face, and he ignored the fact that his hair grew over his collar. He wore his glasses instead of stinging contacts, dressed exclusively in jeans or shorts and old T-shirts, and spent half of every day out on a boat sucking in the salty summer air of King Harbor, where being a Blackthorne was a privilege rather than a "responsibility."

But all that changed when he reached the outskirts of Boston, and especially here at corporate headquarters in the Hancock Tower, where he worked tirelessly to protect and polish the Blackthorne brand. Here—starting again tomorrow morning—he had to be *on*. Shaved, trimmed, suited, tied, and ready to slay the dragons that threatened the family name and business he revered.

Flipping through the stacks of papers his admin had so neatly left in rows on his desk during his three-week absence, he focused on what was ahead for tomorrow, when he'd suit up for his job once again.

Despite the pileup of work, he didn't regret his choice to stay in King Harbor for most of July. And it wasn't like he hadn't worked at all up there. Keeping an eye on Phillip, especially with his oldest brother so deeply involved in that high-profile fund-raiser—and the woman running it—was always a full-time job.

But as July had slipped into August, he'd known he had a few brand management issues to deal with at corporate headquarters, and it wasn't just that someone dropped that pesky "e" into the word whisky where it didn't belong. Although that *would* piss off any Scotsman worth his kilt.

Phillip was under control—thanks to Ashley—but there was still the cloud of... *Claire*. His aunt's sudden decision to abandon the family by waltzing out of her own birthday party, claiming to be the keeper of some big secret, was an image crisis waiting to happen.

Since Brock couldn't do anything from King Harbor to get her back, at least he could be in Boston to manage any bad press or squash any unwanted rumors. Because, with Claire Blackthorne gone for three months, even though Blackthorne Security had tracked her to Paris, people in the company and the industry were bound to gossip.

Was Claire and Graham's marriage on the rocks? Would it affect the company? And what was the secret she'd flung at her husband?

Brock didn't have any answers—his aunt's replies to his texts were brief, airy, and uninformative. But finding answers wasn't his job. His job was to fend off the questions.

So, he'd left Maine late that afternoon, hit wretched Sunday-night traffic as everyone who'd escaped Boston for a blistering summer weekend all returned at the same time, and didn't get to his condo until after eight. Early enough to drop off his bags and walk one mile through oppressive Back Bay humidity to a silent, empty office to ease himself into the work that he faced in the coming week.

And there was plenty of it, he realized as he skimmed the lists and agenda Karen had left. His admin had lined up back-to-back appointments, four lunches, two staff meetings, and one entire day previewing logo misuses and copyright infringements. Monday morning looked busier than usual, starting early with a ten-minute "courtesy session" with J. Gillespie, whoever that was. *Courtesy* usually meant Karen had been pressured into the meeting—sometimes by family, sometimes by outside forces—that she knew Brock didn't want to take.

Then it wouldn't be considered *discourteous* to make Mr. Gillespie conduct his business while Brock's barber came in to give him a haircut and shave to start the week. He texted his admin to add that to his schedule.

Once he finished reviewing everything on his desk, Brock headed out to the private elevator that took occupants of the executive suite down to Clarendon Street, intending to walk back to his condo. But when he stepped out of the elevator, he realized maybe he *should* have looked out the window at least once. Now, he just stared at the city street and let out a soft curse.

Torrential rain turned the pavement black, wet, and slick, while cars sprayed rooster tails as they sped by. His driver, Hoyt, would be home with his family on this weekend night, and Brock wasn't about to yank the man away just because of a rain shower.

Only, this wasn't a rain shower...this was a *downpour*.

He opened the door and winced when rain splattered his T-shirt and jeans and turned his glasses into wet windshields without wipers.

Just as he backed into the building to get an Uber, he spied the white light of an open taxi cruising down Clarendon. Without hesitation, he made a run for it, instantly blinded by sluicing, splashing, relentless water.

Squinting into the rain, Brock saw the cab slow down even before he raised his hand. When the car stopped completely, he jumped a puddle and snagged the passenger-side back door, whipping it open at the very moment that someone did the same to the door on the other side.

"Oh no!" A woman as wet and bedraggled as he was sputtered the exclamation. "Didn't you see me?"

He swiped at his lenses. "Can't see a thing. It's okay," he said, backing away. "You take it."

"No, no. I hailed it, but I guess you technically opened the door first."

"It's fine," he assured her as the water seeped into his docksiders. "I'll catch the next one."

"Tonight?" She slipped into the seat, the light of the cab giving him the first real look at plastered hair and streaky mascara. "We can share. I mean, unless you're a serial killer."

"I can assure you—" A bolt of lightning flashed white and sudden, illuminating a look of shock on her face and giving him a millisecond to see her big blue eyes pop with surprise at the flash. "I'm not a serial killer."

She waved him in. "Quick, then. Get—"

"In or out, buddy," the cabby called in a thick Boston accent, making no effort to hide his exasperation.

"I'm only going to the Colonnade Hotel," the woman said, blinking away some water. "Please get in out of the storm."

Making a snap decision spurred by the cold rain soaking through his shirt and shoes, as well as the tantalizing spark in her eyes, he climbed into the cab and pulled the door closed.

"One Dalton," he said to the driver. "But take this lady wherever she wants to go first. I'll pay."

"That's not—"

He held up a hand. "Please. It's the least I can do to be saved from drowning."

She gave him a smile, but the inside of the cab was too dim for him to take a better, longer look. He caught a whiff of something fresh and floral and noticed she wore a skirt or dress—something that had ridden up high enough to show half a bare thigh—toned, tight, and wet from rain.

"It was clear skies when I left New York." She scooped up a handful of what was probably light blond, but soaking wet, hair and squeezed it so some water dribbled down her top.

"It was clear skies an hour ago when I left home." He threw her another look as the cabby cut off a van to get back into traffic. "You from New York?" he asked.

"I am, but I'm in Boston on business. I take it you're a local?"

"Born and raised." A lifetime of self-protection adopted by anyone saddled with a recognizable last name prevented him from saying more, but he could feel her curious gaze on him.

"Where's your Boston accent?"

"I travel a lot," he said quickly. "Where's your New York accent?"

"My mother was in television and insisted I lose it," she told him with just enough of a smile for him to notice how attractive she was, despite what the weather had done to her hair and makeup.

He let his gaze linger a moment, then asked, "So what brings you out on a night like this?"

She squished her nose as if she didn't really want to say why she was there. "Had to…get the lay of the land." Her tone was vague enough to be intriguing. That bare thigh was intriguing, too, come to think of it.

"What business are you in?" he asked, wanting to keep the conversation going.

"Publishing." The single-word answer trumpeted disinterest—or a plea for privacy—so he nodded and tried to look out his window, but sheets of rain blocked any view as the driver made a wide right turn onto Stuart.

What the hell? Was this guy's vision more blurred than Brock's? Leaning forward, he peered out the front windshield and frowned. "Hey, man, you're going the wrong way."

"This is fast—oh damn!" the man exclaimed as a set of headlights blinded him.

"It's *one way*," Brock insisted through gritted teeth, gauging the speed and distance of the oncoming car and praying like hell the other driver could see through the shimmering wall of rain.

"I screwed up." The cabby slammed on the brakes, making the back wheels fishtail wildly, knocking the whole back bumper into a mailbox, bringing them to a noisy, sudden stop.

"What the heck?" The woman next to Brock grabbed his arm as the driver swore again.

The oncoming car lay on the horn for a deafening five seconds as it careened by, clipping the side-view mirror and earning a stream of foul language from their driver.

"Whoa, buddy, take it easy." Brock automatically put a calming hand over the one clutching him. "This is why I hate cabs," he muttered, looking around to figure out exactly where they were.

The other car came to a stop as their cabby shoved his door open, letting in a spray of water.

"Good God." Brock and the woman both backed away from the water and sounds of an escalating argument. "This is going south fast."

She shook her head in disbelief. "They're going to fight in this weather?"

"Never underestimate a ticked-off Boston cabby." He was only half kidding, but cringed when the F-bombs started exploding outside. "Want to make a run for it?"

She took less than two seconds to decide, giving him a quick nod in the direction of his door, away from the escalating argument.

"Stay with me." Brock took her hand, wrapping his fingers around her slender ones, and got an unexpected jolt from the touch of wet, warm skin. He tugged her toward the door, flipping the handle, and stepping into yet another three inches of water from Back Bay's notoriously crappy drainage system.

As they ran, another bolt of lightning flashed brightly, making her gasp and stumble. Instantly, Brock put an arm around her and guided her close to a building, under an awning that protected the front door of a bakery. He let the rain hit him, but at least she was somewhat protected.

"Here, there's room," she said, pulling him under the tiny overhang, even though it meant he ended up pressing against her.

"We have to get inside somewhere," he said, looking left and right, partly to get his bearings but mostly because it allowed him to avoid looking right into the eyes of a completely wet stranger less than a centimeter away.

She reached behind her and shimmied the large handle of the glass door. "Locked."

"It's Sunday night," he said, giving up the fight to look down at her.

"We could—" The suggestion was cut off by another bolt of lightning, making her smash her face into his shoulder and muffle a soft scream.

"It's okay," he said, automatically putting his hand on her head. "The storm isn't that close."

Slowly, she pulled back with an embarrassed laugh. "I hate lightning. Hate storms." She squeezed his arms as a rumble of thunder punctuated her announcement. "Hate."

"Got it." He did get it, too. Storms certainly didn't bother him, but he felt the same kind of stress on bridges and in skyscrapers and, hell, the widow's walk at the estate. He used his forearm to wipe water off his glasses so he could get his bearings of the neighborhood. "Okay, there's an Irish pub on that corner," he said, thinking of a place that Blackthorne employees were known to frequent after work. "Can you make it?"

"If we don't get struck by lightning." She bit her lip and blinked more water out of her eyes, suddenly looking incredibly…beautiful. Drenched, scared, but something about her reached into him and flicked a switch that sent way too much juice firing through him.

"I won't let you get struck by lightning," he said under his breath.

Her expression softened, and her eyes widened just a tiny little bit like she'd been struck by a whole different kind of lightning. "You can't promise that," she whispered.

But in that single, crazy flash of an instant, he wanted to promise her…something. A kiss, a touch, more time in the rain.

"How about a drink if we make it to safety? I can promise that."

She gave in to a slow smile that showed some dimples and genuine interest. "Yes, please."

He studied her for a moment, knowing all too well that Brock Blackthorne, keeper of an untarnished reputation, didn't hook up with sexy strangers he'd met in the back of a cab. But tonight, in the rain, with the freedom of Maine still clinging to him and the constraints of his Boston life still one more night away…well, this was a hell of a good way to end the week.

Just then, another bolt of lightning lit the night sky, making her squeeze her eyes shut and let out a squeal. "If we live that long."

He chuckled and eased her a little closer, hyperaware of every curve as she pressed into him. "No more than a hundred and fifty steps," he said. "Don't let go, and I promise you that lightning is ten miles away. Ready?"

"As I'll ever be."

"Three…two…"

"One!" She wrapped her arm around him, and they took off, the rain like curtains of water in their faces, making them both gasp a little for air and laugh and tighten their grip around each other.

They leaped over a puddle, stepped to the side when a car rumbled by to make things worse, and finally reached a door with the requisite shamrock etched in frosted glass.

Brock pushed it open, and a blast of air-conditioning and the smell of beer and corned beef wafted out, along with the noise of a crowded restaurant and a bar packed with locals watching a Red Sox game.

But it was blissfully dry, and they both stood in the vestibule, dripping, staring, and, suddenly, laughing.

"We survived to tell the tale," she announced, throwing her drenched head back with a musical giggle.

"A couple of Boston rats nearly drowned, but not..." He leaned closer to whisper in her ear. "Struck by lightning."

She gave him a look that was no less meaningful even with her streaks of mascara. "Struck by *something*."

That was for damn sure.

He just held her gaze for a few heartbeats, both of them completely still except for the rise and fall of their chests as they caught their breath after the run. And in those few seconds, his whole world seemed to shift a little. Everything felt off-kilter and unbalanced and...warm.

She let out a little sigh and inched away. "I think I'll find a ladies' room," she said, finally looking away from him.

"Yeah, it's...there." He spotted the sign toward the back of the restaurant on the opposite side of the bar. When she turned her head to follow his gesture, he let his gaze slide away from her high cheekbones and shapely lips to appreciate the way a yellow cotton dress stuck to every delicious inch of her.

As she turned back, he looked up, but he knew from the glimmer in her eyes, she'd caught him. "Maybe I'll just stand under the hand dryer for an hour," she said with a dry laugh.

He managed a smile, not bothering to act like he hadn't been looking. "Not on my account."

That made her laugh again as she stepped away and pointed to his chest, then let her finger slowly go south. "You're just as wet…*Harvard*."

He plucked at the decade-old T-shirt he wore with his alma mater's famous emblem, feeling a smile pull. "I hadn't even noticed."

She backed a step away, still holding his gaze. "What's your name, by the way?" she asked.

He almost told her the truth. Almost. But Brock was an unusual name, and women frequently changed if they knew the last name that went with it. He didn't want anything about this encounter to change.

"David," he said easily, using his common middle name, as he often did with strangers. But once he knew her—if he ever knew her—he'd tell her his real name.

"I'm Jenna." She gave a little wave and then held up a finger. "One minute. I'll be right back."

"I'll be waiting." Watching her walk away, he realized that maybe coming back to Boston could be nice and easy after all.

Chapter Two

J enna slipped into the bathroom, took a shaky, ragged breath, and closed her eyes before she looked in the mirror. She didn't want to ruin that delicious, flirtatious, unexpected moment with the reality of what the rain had done to her hair, makeup, and clothes.

But…*David*. He was true to his name—a work of art. Made even more attractive by long dark hair and a scruffy beard and the professorial glasses around dark eyes that melted her with one blistering look. Even the Ivy League T-shirt was cute.

Cute? No, that guy sailed past cute when he got into the cab and insisted on paying. Then he slid right into adorable when he tried to protect her from lightning. And when he peeled that Harvard emblem away from the well-defined cuts of a broad chest and six-pack? Yeah, that was one smoking-hot stranger waiting to have drinks with her out there. Drinks and…

She opened her eyes and cringed at the sight in the mirror.

Surely he couldn't be hitting on *that*.

Leaning in for a closer examination, all she could do was moan at the rivers of mascara. "Urban Decay," she muttered. "You can say that again." Her normally pale blond hair was now the color of a wet rat, flattened to her head and spiraling in dripping curls over her shoulders.

She twisted the water faucet, loaded her palm with foamy hand soap, and scrubbed her face clean. After she dried it with paper towels, she pulled her hair straight back off her face and wrapped the ponytail with a hair tie she had on her wrist.

The clean face and schoolteacher hair pretty much guaranteed that she'd get carded despite her twenty-seven years *and* David in the Rain wasn't going to make a move on her tonight.

Which was…a shame. Not that a hookup with a stranger was in her wheelhouse, but *that* stranger? In a city where no one knew her? After her last project tanked, her career was on life support, and being told by her mother that, once again, Jenna Gillespie was a disappointment?

Oh yeah. A little David in the Rain was exactly what the doctor ordered tonight, no matter where it led.

She stepped back from the mirror to examine her yellow Gap T-shirt dress, barking a laugh. "Oh God." She might as well be naked. No wonder he'd looked at her like…well, like she was naked.

Her stomach tingled at the memory of the heat in his eyes when she'd caught him checking her out, the hint of a smile kicking up one corner of his mouth under that facial hair that was not quite a beard, but not that fake scruff thing that some guys did, either. Whatever it was…it might leave a little burn in its wake.

"Whoa, Jenna May Gillespie. *Settle down.*"

But nothing in her was settled. Nothing.

She pulled the dress from her skin just as the door

popped open, and two women shouldered their way in, heads close in conversation and laughter.

With no desire to make even small talk, Jenna slipped into an open stall and closed the door.

"I still can't believe what I just saw," one said excitedly. "If I didn't think it could get me fired, I'd take a picture to share with the rest of the girls in accounting tomorrow."

"No kidding." The other stall door opened and closed with a solid push. "For a minute, I didn't even know that was Brock."

Brock? Did that girl just say *Brock*? The head of brand management for Blackthorne Enterprises? The very gatekeeper she had to impress tomorrow morning? How many Brocks could there be? Here, in the same neighborhood as the office she'd just scoped out to be sure she knew where she was going tomorrow morning?

She stifled a grunt at the thought of being seen by him, soaking wet and flirting with a complete stranger in a bar, and then having to make her case to the famously uptight Brock Blackthorne tomorrow. She wasn't even sure what he looked like, since all those Blackthornes looked so similar, with their square jaws and dark eyes oozing pride and whiskey. No, no. *Whisky. Use an e, and Brock will ice you out*, someone had warned her.

Was David worth the risk?

"Gotta say he looked hot, though," said the woman using the stall next to Jenna.

"Easy, Olivia. You have about as much chance with a Blackthorne as I do with a Hemsworth."

The laughter was lost on Jenna as she let out a sigh. Brock Blackthorne *was* out there, in the bar, maybe sitting at the table next to hers. The very man who currently held her career in his hands, whether he knew it or not, or she liked it or not.

"But, whoa, that weekend look," the woman in the stall crooned. "Mama *like*."

The other one giggled. "I've heard rumors that he has a Blackthorne logo tattooed on his…" She snorted a laugh. "Maybe the thistle and barrel he's always sending memos about stretches to full size when—"

"*Olivia!*" The other woman punctuated her warning with a toilet flush.

But Jenna just closed her eyes and stifled a grunt of frustration. She had to end this pleasant little interlude and get out of this bar so she didn't come face-to-face with the man who, at this precarious moment in her career, had so much power over her.

Damn it! She hated Brock Blackthorne, and she hadn't even met him yet.

"Come on," Olivia said over the sound of sink water running. "Let's go walk by him and see if he recognizes the underlings."

"Not a chance," the other one replied. "I don't know what brought him down from Mount Blackthorne into this dive on a Sunday night, but it sure isn't so he can pick up a local."

"Right? This place is so lowbrow, they don't even serve Blackthorne here."

Then why was he here ruining Jenna's fantasy night?

It didn't matter. She had to get out of here.

She stayed in the bathroom long enough to call an Uber, not wanting David to try to talk her out of leaving.

Two minutes later, she walked out and scanned the tables and booths for the clean-cut, handsome Brock Blackthorne she'd seen in photos. But her gaze landed on…David.

He sat in a corner booth with two drinks in front of him, his hair a little drier now, but still tousled, with one lock falling close to those sexy glasses. When he saw her, he gave that little half smile with enough smolder in his eyes to know they were both having the same thoughts about this.

He searched her face as she approached, and his smile faded, almost as if he knew something had changed. Well, the Urban Decay had washed off, and maybe he was disappointed as she got closer.

"I hope you don't mind." He gestured toward the drinks. "I ordered the best they have, which, I have to say, isn't that great."

She gave a longing glance to the glasses that held something the color of iced tea, but was probably much stronger.

"Look, I hate to say this, but…" She nibbled her lip and slipped onto the edge of the seat across from him, not committing to fully sitting down. "I have to go."

A frown tugged. "Okay." He drew the word out with just enough disappointment to make her want to cry. "Is it something I said or did?"

She glanced at the room again. Not all the tables were visible, and she didn't see any man who looked remotely like those publicity shots on the Blackthorne Enterprises website, but he could be right behind her for all she knew. "No, no. I just got an emergency text." The lie tasted like crap on her lips.

"You can take a call here," he said. "I don't care."

She shook her head. "I—I can't. I'm sorry."

Very slowly, a knowing smile threatened as he stood. "You're chickening out."

"Not…no. Not exactly."

"I can tell you're not the type to…" He made a face

16

that kind of said it all. "I'm not really, either, truth be told."

She sighed out a breath. "I might have been," she admitted on a whisper. "You're really nice, David."

He flinched a little, like a man who just found out he'd almost had a great night. "So are you, Jenna." Standing slowly, he angled his head. "How long are you in Boston?"

It all depended on how that meeting went tomorrow. She slid a glance to a tall guy at the bar, but his hair was too light and long to be the corporate stiff that Brock was purported to be.

"A few more days," she said, looking up at him, appreciating that V-shape of a broad torso and narrow hips. God, she wanted to rip that Harvard T-shirt off. With her *teeth*. "Assuming things go well with my project."

"How about we have dinner tomorrow night?"

An unexpected rush hit her chest. "I'd love that."

"The Colonnade, right? I'll pick you up at seven?"

"I'll be in the lobby."

"Great."

She started to stand, but he held up a hand, then slipped the other in his pocket for a phone. "Let me get you an Uber. Even if the rain stopped, it's a long walk."

"I just called one," she said, turning her phone over to check the app. "He'll be here in two minutes."

"Okay." David pulled out his wallet and tossed some money on the table. While he did, Jenna rose and took one more scan of the bar.

"You don't have to go," she said. Maybe he could find other company.

He gave a soft laugh and adjusted his glasses. "This booze isn't worth staying without you."

"Oh." That was so sweet. "But..."

"Don't worry." He put a hand on her back to usher her toward the door. "I want to walk you out." He lowered his head to get his mouth close to her ear. "Gotta have at least one kiss goodbye."

Her whole body tensed and heated at the baritone whisper and how much she wanted that kiss. And more of that sexy voice sending chills up her spine all night long. "Maybe two," she replied, leaning into him a tiny bit.

As they stepped outside, they both laughed and looked up.

"Now it stops," she said, holding her hand out to feel barely a drizzle.

With his hand on her shoulder, he turned her a little to face him. "But as rainstorms go, that one was pretty damn fun."

"Yeah," she said, sounding a little breathless as she locked on to his gaze. "It was."

For a long moment, they just looked at each other, and she felt that same warmth curl through her, but with a little more urgency than before. A little ache started low in her belly as she memorized the lines of his face and the depth of his eyes.

"You sure you have to go?" he asked, sliding his hands around her waist as if it was the most natural thing in the world.

"I had to leave that bar."

"Why?"

She swallowed. "Someone was in there who…" She shook her head, not willing to admit she was afraid of a man she'd never met. "I had to leave."

"Oh, I get it."

He didn't, but let him think it was an ex she wanted to avoid. She glanced over her shoulder for the Uber,

18

wishing like hell the driver would be at least five more minutes so she could stay this close to David's solid, warm body. "Don't worry. If he comes out, I'll cover you."

She smiled. "How?"

He dipped his head. "Like this."

His lips came down on hers, hot and sweet and tasting like rain and maybe whatever was in that glass he'd left behind. She let a moan escape her throat as goose bumps rose over her body, and a little tornado started building between her legs. His tongue traced her teeth as he rubbed his hands up and down her back, every move slow and deliberate and…promising.

The rumble of a car pulled her back into the moment, followed by the soft spray of tires in the gutter next to them.

"Picking up Jenna?"

"Damn it." They whispered the words in perfect unison, right into each other's mouth right before they broke the kiss.

"I'm Jenna." The words came out rough, her breath trapped in her lungs.

David held her a little tighter, as if letting go would physically hurt. "Can I share your Uber?"

The question spilled over her like more rain, hot this time, and welcome.

"Yeah." She didn't want to give it too much thought. Didn't want to analyze and paralyze. All she wanted was to go with the moment…and with David.

He opened the door for her, then slid in after. "The Colonnade Hotel?" It was as much a question to her as an instruction to the driver.

And as soon as the car moved, David pulled her closer, smoking her with one long look. "Five more minutes," he whispered. "Better make the most of them."

She closed her eyes and slid into another hot kiss, as dizzy as if she'd downed both those glasses left on the table. She wrapped her arms around him, tucking herself into his body for the sheer pleasure of it.

With a sweet sigh into her mouth, he slid his hand up and down her waist, slipping to the front, grazing her breast with a sure, talented touch. "What do you want, pretty, pretty Jenna?"

She eased back to open her eyes and look at him. What did she want? Distraction? Escape? A night not to worry about tomorrow but to give in to what her body was screaming for?

"This." She lifted her head and let his lips sear her throat. "That." She arched her back to offer his hand full access to her body. "Everything."

"Everything can be arranged." On the next kiss, he slid his tongue into her mouth to make her whole body quake with need. "You sure you want to go to your hotel, or would you like to visit my place?"

His place. That was…a little too real. "I have an early meeting."

"So do I." He kissed her lightly, as if he sensed her trepidation. "The Colonnade it is."

"Yes." Hotel sex with a stranger was…not fine, exactly. But what she needed.

With her career on the line and her life on the brink of a solid failure, she needed comfort and warmth and a mouth that made her forget everything for just one night.

Tomorrow, she'd fight her battles with Brock Blackthorne. Tonight, she'd give in to the raw, rugged promise of David in the Rain.

Chapter Three

"Whoa. Whoa. Holy…*whoa*."

"Whoa…what?" Brock looked up from his desk, pulling his thoughts away from the night before, to meet the familiar gaze of a woman he trusted as much as any other in his life. Familiar and, this morning, shocked.

"That's quite the fur coat you're growing on your face."

He rubbed his beard. "Almost four weeks in King Harbor."

"One more, and you'll need a weed wacker to brush your teeth."

He laughed and shook his head, always amused by Karen Whitmeyer, who'd been his administrative assistant since he first walked into this office, fresh out of business school, five years ago. "No one complained…" *Last night.* "In Maine."

"Well, your eight-thirty meeting just arrived in the lobby. But Duke is on his way up to cut your hair and do something about that…" She tipped her head, scrutinizing him with her keen maternal size-up that she probably gave to her teenagers when they came down for breakfast every morning. "Normally, I don't like a beard on you, but with that Armani? Something's working on you today."

Something worked on him last night. "Yeah, well, I feel good. Maine always does that to me." And a woman with the sweetest lips, the sexiest body, and a surprisingly adventurous spirit. Just the thought of Jenna in his arms all night until he had to slip out at six that morning brought a smile to his face.

"You certainly look…" She crossed her arms and studied him again. "I don't quite know how to describe it."

Satisfied. Charged. Ready for more tonight when he would pick her up at seven. He gave a sly smile. "I met someone, all right?"

She sucked in a breath. "In Maine?"

"Actually, right here in Boston."

"Oh my word." She pressed the files she was holding to her chest like he'd just given her the secret to a happy life. "My prayers have been answered, Brock."

If she'd been praying for him to have the best sex in memory, yeah. But something told him this churchgoing woman hadn't exactly been praying for that.

"Tell me about her."

"More later." If he told her too much, shrewd Karen would sniff out the circumstances of last night's hookup in no time. "We have a date tonight, and we'll see how it goes. For now, let's work." He moved the papers on his desk to get her attention there.

"Can't you tell me anything about her? Name, rank, and how ready for marriage?"

"Work, Karen." He tapped the open calendar. "Starting with Mr. Gillespie. I have zero idea what he wants or why you set up a courtesy session, so color me unprepared, which is why I'm sure you're here, not just to dig into my love life or pass judgment on my five-o'clock shadow."

"Honey, that's not a shadow. Two more weeks in Maine and you could audition for *Duck Dynasty*."

"Hardly." He rubbed the facial hair, thinking of how Jenna had said it was like sleeping with Jake Gyllenhaal. He wasn't exactly sure who that was, but she seemed to like the idea.

Karen walked around his desk, dropping a file folder in front of him and heading to the window to separate the blinds and steal a peek as she always did. But she never pestered him to open the blinds to a view that most people would kill for. Karen knew how he felt about looking down fifty-three dizzying floors.

"First of all, your meeting is with *Ms*. Gillespie," she said. "Second, you agreed to the meeting last April, when Oliver Hazlett, senior publisher at Filmore & Fine Publishing, contacted you directly and asked for it."

He frowned and flipped open the file to read the first line of a letter that now looked vaguely familiar. "'The untold story of the Blackthorne family'?" He inched back and gave Karen a look of pure disgust. "Was I *drunk*?"

"Mr. Hazlett golfs with your uncle Graham." She left the window and came back to attend to his out-box. "Does it need more explanation than that?"

No. Graham must have given his approval for this to happen. "And no one crosses Graham Blackthorne," Brock noted. "Except, of course, my aunt." Who hadn't yet flounced off to Europe when Brock had agreed to meet a biographer.

Karen slipped into a guest chair. "I take it there's no word on Claire's, uh, sudden departure?"

He gave his head a slow shake. "She's still in Paris,

and Graham's firmly planted in denial," he said, thinking of how his uncle had been even more gruff than usual when they ran into each other this past month. "You'd think with the way romance has been burning through the Blackthornes this summer, Graham might want to spread a little of that his wife's way."

"I heard about Phillip and Ashley," she said, waggling her brows.

"Now that was a thing of beauty." He grinned. "She took my brother down without much of a fight, I gotta say."

"Happy for him. How about Devlin and Hannah? Still good?"

"Glued together since the race on Memorial Day."

"And Ross?"

"Oh yeah. He's announced he's staying in Kentucky with Holly by his side."

"Who would have thought that they'd all fall in love one right after the other?" She laughed. "Oh, don't forget Jason."

"How could we? He and Mallory are hard at work on his next show, and when she's not in the director's chair, she's in his…" He almost said *bed*. "Arms."

Karen pressed her hands together and pretended to swoon. "It's all so romantic."

"Not all of it. Not this…this rift between my aunt and uncle." He closed his eyes, thinking of the dark cloud that hung over the family despite his brothers and cousins falling hard for great women. "If major accounts or key customers get wind of how serious this is, or how long she's been gone, or…"

"The fact that the Blackthorne family might no longer be able to claim it has been divorce-free for two hundred years? I know you like to slip that in to some of the marketing brochures because it underscores the stability of the brand."

He let out a soft grunt. "It had to happen someday, but…" Not to the two people who'd swooped in and made sure he wasn't an orphan for a single moment after his parents died. Because of Graham and Claire, Brock's childhood was whole and secure, when it could have been anything but after the plane crash that took Julie and Mark Blackthorne from this world.

"I know, I know what you're thinking," Karen said, though she probably didn't. "If the gossip-happy industry rags get hold of this news, it could hurt the value of the company and the brand." She added a smile. "I know what you worry about, Brock."

The brand? A reasonable amount, considering he was the head of brand management for Blackthorne Enterprises. But he worried about the family name and reputation a hell of a lot more. He'd do whatever was necessary to make sure that name was never blemished, wrecked, or disrespected.

"You still have no idea what secret she was referring to?" At his surprised look, Karen added an unapologetic shrug. "Brock, a lot of people overheard that argument at her birthday party, and rumors spread like wildfire around here. You're fooling yourself if you think people who track the highs and lows of the Blackthorne clan aren't trying to figure out what your aunt was talking about when she said she'd kept Graham's secret."

No, he knew the powder keg he was sitting on. "I've been keeping my ear to the ground, and I've heard the conjecture. No one has hit on anything that qualifies as a deep, dark skeleton in our closet."

He closed his eyes to remember the scene again and the fire in his aunt's eyes when she delivered her speech.

"Whatever it is, if and when it comes out, you're right about one thing. I'm the one who has to think about what it could do to the brand. After all, this is the family tree that hasn't had a broken branch in two hundred years. The company is built on the deep roots of that tree. The promise that our products are made with a spirit of unity and quality and—"

"A time-tested tradition aged in oak and pride," she completed the litany of lines straight from the latest brochure in a singsong voice. "Remember, I proof all the marketing materials. And you stress too much."

"Because it matters to me, Karen." He slapped the file in front of him and shoved it across the desk. "Which is why I am not authorizing some trashy tell-all looking to dig up dirt. The Blackthornes have never authorized a single memoir or personal narrative or biopic of any kind, and God knows we're not about to start now."

"Unauthorized biographies have been published."

"Utter trash full of holes, innuendo, and debunked myths," he countered. "So, send in Ms. Gillespie, and I'll tell her we can't help her."

"And the senior publisher at Filmore & Fine? You want to call Mr. Hazlett, or should I talk to Graham's admin about it?"

"God, no. I'll handle him. I'll quietly suggest that if this Gillespie woman goes forward with an unauthorized bio, we'll tie the publisher up in court for so long, they'll pay more in legal fees than they'd ever make on the book."

Karen took the file. "Or you could authorize it," she said in that quiet voice that often hid the smartest advice he got from anyone on his vast marketing team. "That way, you'd control every interview she does, and you could insist on final approval before a single word is ever printed. You could steer her clear of certain topics."

He considered that for about a nanosecond, then dismissed the idea as a time, money, and energy suck. "I have too much work on my plate that takes precedence over some dumb book that won't sell a damn bottle of whisky even if it's the most flattering puff piece ever written. The whole idea is a headache, a nuisance, and a massive risk. I want nothing to do with this...whatever her name is."

"Jenna Gillespie."

"Je..." He felt a frown form. "Jenna?"

"That's her first name. Why?"

The very first tendril of concern wormed its way up his chest. The echo of his own voice whispering that name when they were...

Oh man. That couldn't be possible. "It's not...that common a name," he said to himself as much as to Karen.

"She's not that common a woman," Karen said as she gathered her papers and stood. "She's a beauty, with a sweet smile, warm blue eyes, and quite a lovely figure, not that it matters."

Check, check, check, and oh shit.

"And if you read the rest of that letter, you'll see she's the daughter of the legendary Sam Gillespie, former editor in chief of *The New York Times*, and Charlotte May."

"Char May? Of *60 Minutes*?"

My mother was in television... He stared at Karen in speechless disbelief.

"Retired, now, but yes. Celebrity interviewer extraordinaire. This young lady comes from solid publishing pedigree, and I'd bet there are high expectations on this project."

Publishing. In town on business At Hancock Tower... *to get the lay of the land.* With each remembered phrase, he put the pieces together, and the picture did *not* look good. He'd slept with this woman who wanted to...

"Brock, what's the matter?"

Everything. "This...Jenna. Is she..." *Gorgeous? Witty? Sexy and sweet and freakishly afraid of storms?* "Blond?"

She inched back at the question. "Why don't I just bring her in here, and you can meet her?" She glanced at her phone as she emptied the last of the papers from his out-basket. "Oh, reception just notified me that Duke is here to cut your hair. I'll tell Ms. Gillespie she has ten minutes, max. Knowing you, it'll take two. Should I hold off Duke until you're done with her?"

Done with her? He'd known the minute he said goodbye this morning he wasn't done with her. She was different. Funny. Thrilling. Enticing. And she thought his name was...*David*.

Oh, this was not good. But he sure as hell wasn't going to date the biographer he planned to send home holding nothing but a warning that there could be lawsuits if she proceeded.

Time to break the news...and the date. "I'll see her," he said, unable to hide the disappointment in his voice.

"And Duke? He won't wait more than fifteen minutes before he triple-charges and then has a hissy fit and tells all his customers that Blackthornes are selfish, proud, and their hair grows too fast."

"We are proud." He stabbed his hand into that too-long hair and pulled it back. "Send her in and give Duke a bottle of Blackthorne Gold if he has to wait, but I'm sure this won't take long." Because the minute she saw him, she'd...

What *would* she do? Run? Yell? Laugh it off and beg for more?

Hey, a man could hope.

"Got it, boss." She gave a playful salute and stepped out, leaving Brock to wait. He stood, buttoned his single-breasted jacket, came around the desk, and prayed like hell this was a different Jenna.

But then the door opened, and he stared straight into the beautiful blue eyes of the woman he'd woken up next to this morning. And watched them turn to ice as Karen launched an introduction.

"Brock, this is—"

"*What?*" Jenna choked the word, eyes popping wide, jaw falling open, and every drop of color draining from her cheeks.

He took a step forward. "Hello, Jenna. Nice to, uh, see you again."

She stood frozen in place, gaping at him.

"Uh, I guess you two..." Karen backed away. "I'll leave now."

The sound of the door latching was the only noise in the room. Unless the steam he imagined was coming out of Jenna's ears hissed. No, that was her taking her next breath, nostrils flaring.

"You son of a—"

"Wait. Wait." He held out his hands. "We made a mistake—"

"You can freaking say that again."

"No, *that* wasn't a mistake, but I—"

"Lied about your name." She spat the words at him, taking a step backward as if it all hit her too hard. "You *lied.*"

He shook his head. "I frequently use my middle name when—"

"When seducing strangers."

He hadn't really…okay, he had. But the road to seduction had been a two-way street. "I planned to tell you tonight," he said simply. "I use the name David because my real name attracts attention."

She crossed her arms, glaring at him, all the warmth he remembered from last night and this morning completely gone. "Well, you certainly attracted mine. *David*."

He blew out a breath and rubbed the beard that for some reason had started to itch. "I apologize if you feel deceived, but I had no idea who…what…you are."

Her eyes flashed, but she stayed silent, letting him dig himself deeper.

"You were barely awake when I left, so I figured I'd tell you tonight."

He could see her regain her balance, straightening her shoulders and lifting a defiant chin. "I was awake enough to have sex with you."

He swallowed. "I would hope so."

"I was alert enough to finalize a date."

"Which I was…" *Weirdly happy about.* "Looking forward to."

"And yet, you couldn't manage to whisper, 'Oh, by the way, my real name isn't David' in my ear before you left."

"I whispered in your ear," he said softly. "I'm pretty sure you heard what I said."

Color returned to her face, confirming she most definitely heard his sexy parting shot.

"That was before I knew you were Brock Blackthorne in disguise."

"Disguise?" He touched his face again. "Not exactly."

30

"Beard? Long hair? Glasses? Nothing about you…" She drew back, looked him up and down, lingering on his suit and tie. "Yeah. I guess I see it now. I guess…lust is blind, because I wouldn't have even talked to you had I known who you were."

For some reason, that hurt. "Then see how wrong you can be about people?"

She launched a brow north. "Wrong? You do realize that you are the reason I left the bar?" At his confused look, she added, "Some of your employees announced in the bathroom that Brock Blackthorne was in the building, which meant I had to get out of it."

He fought a little smile at the irony that her running *from* him had taken her right *to* him. But he knew better than to look smug or victorious over that.

Neither one of them said a word for the span of about five long heartbeats. He took the time to drink in every fine feature, the way makeup brought out the beauty of her eyes, and the silky blond hair that had tickled him when she was on top of him the night before.

At the image of her naked in bed, bathed with sweat and pleasure, he closed his eyes. That wasn't going to go away from his brain for a long time, which meant…this situation was one hot, awkward mess.

He blew out a breath and tried to be normal about it. "So, my assistant tells me you're working on a book…" When she didn't move, he gestured to the chair. "Would you like to tell me about it?"

"Not really," she replied, staying exactly where she was. "I'm sure it's a moot point now."

It was a moot point because he had no intention of letting her write this book, but the minute he said that, any chance with Jenna would be gone. And for some reason he didn't understand, he refused to let that happen.

"Not necessarily," he heard himself say. "I don't see why what…transpired…last night should affect business."

The slightest smile kicked up her pretty lips. "What *transpired*, Brock David Blackthorne, was earth-shattering, mind-blowing, toe-curling sex."

With each word, heat crawled up him. And made him want more. "No argument there."

"And now that we've done that, I'm sure you're going to say you can't help me."

He'd planned to say exactly that. But now, he'd just seal his fate as a world-class douche if he sent her off and then called her publisher to threaten a lawsuit. Plus, he didn't *want* to close the door on Jenna Gillespie.

"What kind of help are you looking for?" he asked, knowing it was futile to hope she wanted something simple, like a product sampling or a questionnaire he could answer in writing.

"I need unfettered access to your family, the history, and business of all things Blackthorne. I want private tours, intimate interviews, and behind-the-scenes insights to every aspect of the Blackthorne family."

Brock blinked at her. *Seriously?*

She laughed softly, obviously interpreting his silent, stunned response. "It's fine. I can find the people I need to interview and do it the hard way. My publisher encouraged me to contact you as the gatekeeper, but I can find my way through those gates alone." She turned to the door. "Thank you."

"No." He closed the space between them and put a light hand on her shoulder, instantly jolted by the familiar feel of her and the flowery scent that he now knew was from her shampoo. "Wait, Jenna. Please."

She turned slowly, looking up at him with a question in her eyes. "Yes?"

For a long time, he just stared at her. And the longer he did, the easier this decision was. Yes, he wanted to control this process from beginning to end. Yes, he wanted to be sure that anything written reflected well on the family name he loved and protected.

But that wasn't why he was about to make a decision that went counter to everything that made Brock Blackthorne who he was.

He liked this woman. A *lot*. So, turning into her all-day—and all-night—escort through the interview process didn't seem like the worst idea in the world.

"Give me the day to clear my calendar," he said. "And I'm all yours."

She narrowed her eyes. "On one condition."

He almost laughed. She was doling out conditions? "What's that?"

"You never lie to me again, Brock Blackthorne."

He extended his hand to her. "You have my word."

She took his hand slowly, slipping her much smaller one against his palm. Just then, his door inched open, and Karen peeked in, eyeing their joined hands, then meeting Brock's gaze with a look of hope and interest so utterly Karen-like, he almost laughed.

"Excuse me, Mr. Blackthorne, but how much longer should I tell Duke he can expect to wait?" she asked in her formal admin voice.

"One minute, Karen." When she closed the door, he finally let go of Jenna's hand, but stayed just inches from her. "I have an appointment with my barber," he said to her. "We can start over dinner tonight? That is, if you don't have plans."

"I had plans with David," she said, letting her gaze drop over his face, then down to the suit and tie he wore.

"But it looks like his barber is about to eliminate every last shred of him."

"Same guy, different hair."

"And now you're Brock, so that changes everything."

"Everything?"

"Listen to me." She reached up and straightened what he knew was a perfectly straight tie, looking at his neck, then slowly gazing up into his eyes. "The fact is, I've been burned by a source recently. Another gatekeeper who lied to me." She sighed, shuddering slightly at the admission. "And you should know that my entire career is riding on this book proposal, along with a lot of money, a shredded reputation, and the opinions of people I love. I'm not going to mess with it by..." She swallowed, lifting a brow that said so much more than words could, reluctantly letting go of his tie.

That was a no-more-sex brow if he ever saw one.

"I won't sleep with Brock Blackthorne," she confirmed. "It would go against every professional ethic there is."

Disappointment thudded while a few thousand hormones groaned in defeat. "Maybe David will make a reappearance," he teased.

"Won't matter. One night will have to have been enough for us."

He watched her leave, putting a hand on the tie knot she'd just touched, knowing deep in his gut that one night was not going to be enough. Not by a long shot.

Chapter Four

"All right, Char, I have to go. My meeting is starting in two minutes," Jenna said into the cell phone balanced precariously on the bathroom sink while she leaned toward the mirror and added a dab of lipstick as a finishing touch.

Meeting. Not a *date*. It might have been at one time, a thousand years and twenty-four hours ago, but it wasn't anymore. There'd be no longing gazes across the table, no accidental hand brushes, and no head-banging sex.

"Just remember, Jenna," her mother continued. "The question you don't ask is as important as the one you do."

Yeah, like last night, when it never occurred to her to ask, *Do you know Brock Blackthorne? You see him anywhere in this bar?*

"I'll remember, Char," she promised her mother, whose broadcasting-trained voice was also the voice of wisdom, experience, guidance, and—

"So, for God's sake, don't blow it again."

And, sometimes, *disappointment*. "Thanks for that vote of confidence, Mother Dearest."

She snorted softly. "Hey, I'm the one who believes in what you're doing. Your father…" Her voice drifted off.

"How is he?" Jenna asked.

"Old," she replied on a laugh. "But then, we both are."

The fact was, Char May had been forty-one when Jenna was so unexpectedly conceived, and her father, a shocking fifty-six. Childless for their entire marriage and stellar careers, they'd approached parenthood as if their new arrival was another agenda item on their busy schedules.

"I meant after the hip surgery," Jenna said.

"Oh Lord, nothing stops that man. Not even a titanium ball and socket. But he's worried about you, Jenna. That last book situation…" She sighed, and Jenna could just hear the whoosh of her caftan when she picked up that martini glass again. "It was a disaster, honey."

The term of endearment didn't do anything to take the punch out of the words. Yes, the first book in Jenna's two-book deal with Filmore & Fine had gone south at the most inopportune time—five days before publication.

"How could I know the main source for the most important chapter in the true story of the House of Villeneuve would turn out to be…" She closed her eyes and tried not to picture David. "A liar?" Thinking of him, she tapped the phone to check the time and cringed when she saw it was after seven. David might run a few minutes behind, but Brock Blackthorne would not be late. "And I have to go. I was supposed to be in the lobby five minutes ago."

"Just do your homework earlier and better this time," her mother said, physically incapable of ending a phone call without one more shovelful of advice.

"Don't worry, I have an in at the company now," she

said. An *in* who'd already lied to her, but still… "Anyway, failure is not an option."

"You could always move in with Dad and me and let us take care of you."

Oh Lord. Failure was *so* not an option. "Thanks, but I got this."

"Just remember this, Jenna. Let your source *lead* you to the truth, not *tell* you the truth, because what they say won't be the truth," she continued, clearly spurred on by the gin. "When you want to rip the layers off a subject, you have to do it—"

"*Mother.*" Sometimes she had to break down and not call her by her famous nickname. "I don't want to rip anything off Brock Blackthorne." Except, maybe, his clothes. *Again.*

Which wasn't going to happen if she had a snowball's chance of succeeding and gaining career redemption after the book that crashed and burned.

But she had one more chance. Filmore & Fine had given her an impossible task, but she wouldn't stumble. Especially because a screwup would mean she'd have to pay back the advance, which would mean…

Hello, Mother. Hello, Father. Here's your millennial failure looking for a place to live.

"I *have* to go," Jenna said quickly, grabbing the phone and heading out of the bathroom. "I'll talk to you soon. Maybe later. Maybe in a week. Bye!"

Before her mother could dish out one last closing comment, Jenna disconnected, dropped the phone in her bag, and snagged the room key from the dresser.

"Here goes nothing," she whispered as she stepped into the dimly lit hallway and then into the elevator. This time, it could be different. This time, it could be better. This time, it could be…

Hot.

It was the only word that popped into her head when the elevator doors opened, and she saw Brock Blackthorne leaning against the back of a lobby sofa.

And her second thought was...*so hot.*

Great, Jenna. He's killed your words.

If he had, the loss of a few brain cells was understandable. Yeah, David with a wet beard and long hair and a Harvard T-shirt was pretty sexy. But Brock decked out for business was...*not fair.*

He held his suit jacket over his shoulder, hooked on a finger, his white dress shirt tailored to accentuate the breadth of his chest and cut of his biceps. She'd traced every cut of that six-pack...with her tongue.

Damn, this would be so much easier if she didn't already know what she was missing.

"Hey." He pushed off the sofa and took one step, slow enough for her to see his gaze drop over her, lingering on the V in the neck of her black cocktail dress, all the way down to her heels, then back up again, coming to rest on her face.

He'd just totally eye-screwed her and...God help her. She liked it.

"Brock David Blackthorne." She held out her hand to stave off any chance that he'd reach for a hug.

"Jenna May Gillespie." When her eyes widened in surprise, he gave a guilty laugh. "My admin told me that's how you signed in at reception."

Of course, her full name was on her driver's license. Or had he done his research on her? Didn't matter. He was the subject of the interview, not her.

He took her hand, and just as it had every time they'd touched since last night in the cab, electrical currents pirouetted up her arm, through her body, and settled in the most inappropriate place. "You look…" He gave a soft laugh. "Not sure what's appropriate here," he admitted. "Gorgeous? Beautiful in black? Or…"

"How about 'ready to work on the authorized account of the Blackthorne family,'" she finished for him.

"That, too."

"Are we eating here at the hotel?" she asked, nodding to the small and very ordinary lobby dining room. "It'd be fast and easy."

"And subpar." He put a hand on her back and led her to the door. "You want to know how Blackthornes live?"

"I want to know everything," she told him. "So, yes, I want to know how they live."

He reached for the door when the only doorman was preoccupied with another guest. "Boring, that's how we live."

"Not a chance."

"We're just not that fascinating," he said. "The whisky is. The race cars are. And the boats can make you want to chuck life and sail to the ends of the earth. We came in second in the Southern Maine Sailing Invitational in May. Did you know?"

"Second? For some reason, I didn't imagine Blackthornes would be second in anything."

He smiled. "Well, my cousin Devlin lost the race *and* his confirmed bachelor status to the same woman, so we come in second if we want to."

"He threw the race?"

He shrugged. "No one is actually saying."

Outside, they walked under the overhang to a black stretch limo, where a gray-haired man in a suit instantly opened the back door, nodding to her.

"A limo?" she asked, hesitating to get in.

"My uncle wanted the town car I usually use, so we

got an upgrade," he replied, then gave her a teasing nudge. "Unless you want to call our friend the cabby."

She gave a soft sigh as she stepped toward the open door. "You're right. At least your driver won't get into a fistfight."

"You hear that, Hoyt?" he said to the driver. "No fighting tonight."

"No promises, Mr. Blackthorne." The reply came with enough twinkle in Hoyt's gray eyes that Jenna could tell the two men knew each other well. "Things can get pretty hairy with those Menton valets."

Brock laughed, following Jenna into the back seat.

"Menton?" She slid to the side, giving a quick tug to her dress so her entire thigh wasn't exposed. "Even I've heard of that restaurant, and I don't live in Boston."

"Just voted one of the top ten restaurants in the country," he said. "Definitely not the hippest eatery in town, but I love the food and atmosphere, and the chef is a friend."

The confession made her give him a side-eye as she settled into the cool, plush seat and inhaled the lightest mix of leather, woods, and something barely floral. God, even Brock's limo smelled delicious.

"I can't believe you were right in front of my face the whole time and I didn't see you," she admitted on a whisper.

He reached for her hand, and as much as she wanted to whip her fingers away to avoid that zing of his touch again, she didn't. Or couldn't. Instead, she let him take her hand and give it the softest squeeze.

"Will a simple 'I'm sorry' do?"

She studied him for a moment, finally sliding her hand free, although it pained her to do so. "Agreeing to help me goes a long way," she said slowly. "And I understand that some famous people want to hide their identity, but after meeting in the cab like that…"

He turned more toward her, as if sitting side by side just wasn't intimate enough. No, he had to actually melt her with those brown eyes. "I'm just protective of the name and everything attached to it. Also, let's get this straight. I'm not famous."

"Well known? Household name? Insta-worthy?"

He rolled his eyes. "If that's the family you think you're going to write about, you might want to switch your assignment to the Kardashians or…" He lifted a brow. "Villeneuve."

Oh, he *had* done some research. *Damn it.*

"I really had planned to tell you my real name tonight," he said, "before we even left the lobby of your hotel for our date."

"Which is now not a date. It's a meeting. A business meeting between a writer and her source."

"Taking all the fun out of it."

"Depends on how much my source shares," she quipped. "A good interview can be a blast."

"So can…" He searched her face, slightly closer. Not too close, but not exactly on the other side of the car, either. "A thunderstorm and a wild cab ride."

She couldn't help the smile that tugged. "It was fun, I'm not going to lie. But I told you…"

"And I heard you," he assured her, inching away as if that proved he knew his boundaries. "But your reaction proves my point about the name. It comes with baggage. It comes with expectations and preconceived notions."

Now that, her mother would say, was an opening that a biographer needed to kick with her boot and force her way in. Carefully, of course. "Is that a problem you have with women, Brock?"

"I don't have problems with women."

She almost laughed at that. "I bet you don't. But you assume they have expectations about your name. Do you think you might disappoint them? Or that they want something you can't provide? Or that—"

"Don't."

She lifted her brows in question.

"Don't get personal."

"Little late for that," she shot back.

"Hey, you set the ground rules today. If we're not intimate, then we're not personal."

As intense as his gaze was, seeming to look right through her, Jenna refused to look away or accept the order. "Maybe you don't know how this process works, Brock." She leaned toward him to make her point. "The whole idea is that I get personal. Every minute of every interview is personal. How else am I going to find the soft underbelly of the Blackthorne family?"

He closed a little more space between them. "I guarantee you no one in my family has a soft belly."

Oh yes, she remembered.

"Are you telling me," she whispered, "that you won't tell me anything personal?"

"Will *you* tell *me* something personal?"

She hesitated for a moment. "If you haven't already done all your homework on me. Sounds like you have."

"A little," he admitted. "Enough to be thoroughly intrigued."

She narrowed her eyes to make a point he couldn't ignore or flirt away. "You *can't* be anything more than a source for me, Brock."

"No, Brock can't. But David?" He smiled, and something told her that sly grin of his had wooed a lot of women over the years. It changed his face from stoic to sexy and made him relaxed, approachable, and gorgeous. "What if David shows up in the off-hours?"

A thousand chills danced up her spine. "Just wear your glasses, and we'll see."

"Just like Superman and Clark Kent."

She laughed. "*Just.*"

Chapter Five

"Please bring two glasses of Blackthorne Gold, neat," Brock quietly instructed the hostess who seated them at Brock's regular table overlooking Congress Street. But not so quietly that Jenna didn't give him a surprised glance as she settled into the chair he held for her.

"I'll just have water," she said.

He gave her a look that he hoped communicated what he thought of that as he sat down, purposely taking the seat across the small, square table for two.

"Who starts dinner with whisky, anyway?" she asked.

And that earned her another look of sheer disbelief from him, making her laugh.

"I guess I forgot who I'm with."

"Jenna." He took the napkin from the table. "If you're going to learn about Blackthornes, you're going to have to know and love the drink that is synonymous with our name. Not everyone starts dinner with a glass of Gold, but I like to. Plus, I want to tell you about it, and you can't appreciate the history if you don't taste our finest product. It's book research, I swear."

She gave him a smile of surrender. "All right, I'll try it. And I'm sure I'll like it, considering its colorful history."

Its colorful history? He stayed silent, not sure if she'd meant the whole company, the brand, or the premium whisky that some said had a shadowy past.

"But this isn't the kind of place where I can take notes or record you," she added. "So I need to stay clearheaded so I can transcribe everything we discuss into my research tonight. I honestly cannot waste a minute."

"I know," he agreed. "Three weeks is a stunningly short time frame. I'd think you would have more."

She exhaled hotly. "I'm being punished."

"For the Villeneuve book?"

"I thought you were spending the day in all those meetings clearing your calendar, not researching the researcher."

"Karen pulled a few facts for me," he confessed. "And I had a quick call with Oliver Hazlett."

She cringed. "Went straight to my boss at Filmore & Fine, did you?"

He didn't respond as a tuxedoed waiter brought their drinks in heavy crystal glasses, nodding to Brock in that deferential way that said the server knew exactly who was getting their best bourbon.

"The chef is a James Beard winner," Brock told Jenna. "I usually let her surprise me with something called the Chef's Whim, unless you have food allergies or issues."

"Maybe you should ask Karen," she replied with a playful smile. "But no, I'm sure I'll love whatever the chef prepares."

When the waiter left, Brock lifted his glass and waited for her to do the same. "To your success," he said.

"Which, if you talked to my publisher, you probably know is seriously on the line right now." She tapped his glass lightly. "But thank you, and I will certainly drink to that. Anything I should know before my very first sip of Blackthorne whisky, other than no e in whisky?"

He smiled. "Get that right, and you win major points with me," he said. "What you're about to taste is our finest, top-shelf bourbon-style whisky, the only one made in our Maine distillery, from locally grown sugar gold corn, which is where it gets its Blackthorne Gold name." He lifted the glass. "Tradition you can taste." He dragged out the company tag line like an ad exec presenting new creative content.

"Can't wait," she said, bringing the glass closer to her mouth.

"Take it slow. This is probably hotter, stronger, and smoother than anything you've ever had."

"In other words, spewing it all over you would be really bad form."

He laughed. "Wouldn't be the first shot I had to wear home."

Her eyes widened in anticipation as she started to press the glass to her lips. "To my first taste of Blackthorne."

Not exactly her first, but if she wasn't going to flirt about what they'd done last night, then he wouldn't, either. "Enjoy," he said simply, sipping his and watching her, which was more intoxicating than the drink.

She closed her eyes with a low, sweet moan of appreciation. Her throat rose and fell with the swallow, her head tipped slightly back, as she let out a sigh that sounded exactly like the one she'd released when he'd kissed his way from her mouth to her toes.

Arousal threatened, making him shift imperceptibly in his seat. He couldn't spend this whole night warding off his body's natural response to her. Damn. Was it always going to be like this with her?

"Ohhhh." The sound came out as a helpless exclamation that could qualify as one of the sexiest things he'd ever heard. Since last night. "Brock."

Yes. It was *always* going to be this way with her.

He covered by bringing his glass back for one more taste. "Did you get the oak and vanilla?" he asked. "That subtle hint of caramel from the sweet corn? Did you taste that?"

"I tasted…heaven." She lifted the glass to inhale the fragrance, again closing her eyes. "And yes, smoke. And…pleasure. Maybe a little temptation. And a flash of insanity, a moment of madness, and a warm fire on a winter night."

He cracked up. "You're inspiring new ad copy for my marketing team."

"Blackthorne Gold," she said, leaning closer. "It's better than…"

Neither one of them said a word.

"Well, it's almost as good," she finished with a soft laugh.

"That is, if we're going to be honest about the elephant in the room," he said.

She gave him a sharp look, and he could swear he saw a warning in her eyes. Then she let out a sigh. "Speaking of elephants in the room…" She swirled the liquid, gazing at it so he could see the way her dark lashes fanned over high cheekbones.

Oh yeah, he thought, taking a drink. This was going to be a long night, and if he didn't start thinking about something else, it was going to end like the last one. Which didn't bother—

"This is so good, it's no wonder Alistair Blackthorne stole the recipe."

He choked on his sip. "*Excuse* me?"

"Please don't act like you're surprised." She lowered the glass, but not all the way, holding it in front of the small candle on the table, letting the light dance through the amber liquid. "They said the golden color of the Salmon Falls whiskey—with an e, I might add—had never been replicated until the Blackthorne family moved to King Harbor from Scotland. Coincidence? Some say yes, some say no."

He stared at her, fighting the rush of resentment as strong as all the other rushes he'd been enjoying the past few moments. God, he hated this old stupid myth that somehow refused to die. "The ones who say no would be correct."

"And the ones who say yes?"

"Would be jealous of our success." He inched the glass away, keeping his gaze on it. "Salmon Falls Distillery closed during Prohibition. It's little more than a pile of bricks and overgrown trees in the middle of the woods."

"And yet, the Blackthorne distilleries…flourish."

He just shrugged, no stranger to the folklore about his great-grandfather and the neighboring distillery. "Alistair Blackthorne was smart and knew how to turn a dime. Lots of liquor companies survived and thrived during Prohibition, and some went out of business."

"Because their top-shelf recipe was replicated by another."

He lifted the glass, feeling his jaw clench. "That's not true, Jenna. This color you see? It's the barrels, which are each aged over a year after being burned with special flames that incorporate distinct flavors in specified amounts. These techniques came from Scotland."

"But this isn't Scotch whisky."

"Of course not. Scotch, by law, can only be made in

Scotland, distilled from barley and the rich peat of the land. Bourbon whisky is made from corn, technically in Bourbon County, Kentucky. Blackthorne bourbon-*style* whisky evolved from a two-hundred-year-old recipe and aging technique that my great-grandfather's family made for private use and then brought from Scotland when he arrived in the United States." He leaned in to add, "He didn't steal it."

She just smiled at him. "Relax. I'll figure it out when I talk to someone who knows the history."

"I know the history."

"The history of Salmon Falls," she shot back. "If it's not true, I'll find that out. I can discern the truth. *David.*"

He winced at the dig.

"And, if your short conversation with my publisher included any details, you know that I am smart enough to know when I'm being lied to." She angled her head with a self-deprecating smile. "Sadly, it took a long time for me to get there on my last project."

"Well, I heard his version. How about you tell me yours?" When she looked down at the whisky and didn't answer, he touched her hand lightly. "So we can avoid the same mistakes."

The waiter came with the amuse-bouche before she could answer, so their conversation stopped to appreciate the tuna crudo with watermelon. Brock asked that the wine director choose their wine and waited until they were completely alone again to finish his whisky and let her do the same.

"If I'm going to be perfectly honest," she finally said, "there was nothing I could have done differently, but I was blindsided by a source. It turned out that the very premise of the biggest reveal in the book was all a lie, but I only discovered the discrepancies after the book had been edited and sent to the printing press. I could have…" She closed her eyes. "No, I *couldn't* have lived with the repercussions if I'd tried to hide what I'd discovered. I had to go to my publisher and tell them to pull the book."

No wonder she was a stickler for a truthful source. "But you're doing another book for them, so it couldn't have been catastrophic."

She gave a wry laugh. "Trust me, it felt like a catastrophe at the time. They're giving me a second chance because it was a two-book contract, but they are under no obligation to accept my proposal. I know they love the idea of a Blackthorne bio, but I'm not sure they love the idea of me writing it. Other than, you know…"

He took a guess. "Your famous pedigree."

Her mirthless smile confirmed his guess was right. "Charlotte May's name carries a lot of weight, and my dad's position at the *Times* made him a lot of friends. But, the business is ruthless and they aren't thrilled with me. If they opt out of this book proposal, I have to pay back the entire advance. Which, I hate to say, is pretty much spent."

"And your parents?"

"Drowning their disappointment in their martinis as we speak."

"Oh, that is a lot of pressure."

She gave a shrug, then eyed him with a dubious look. "And you are very good, Brock Blackthorne."

"How so?"

"I'm the interviewer, yet…" She slid a tiny-pronged fork over a lemon balm on her plate. "You've managed to find out more about me than I have about you, and we're halfway through the first course."

"I don't know much," he said.

"You know that my career is on a downward spiral, my wallet is thin, and my parents think I'm not worthy of their names." She picked up the empty whisky glass. "Truth serum?"

"Nectar of the Blackthorne gods," he replied.

"With a little help from…Wilfred Platt."

"Who the hell is that?"

"The original owner of Salmon Falls Distillery."

He rolled his eyes. "Your time is precious, Jenna. I recommend you don't waste it on what will be a dead end."

She didn't answer right away, enjoying a bite of food and giving him time to study the way her corn-silk-colored hair fell over her cheekbone, accentuating her delicate features and the curve of her lips.

"Another question, then?" she asked.

"Anything."

"Why did you agree to help me? You know there isn't going to be a…repeat performance of last night. You could have closed the door and let me ferret out my own information and stumble through the Blackthorne Enterprises machine, which would have slowed me down and perhaps killed the book."

"It's a fair question," he agreed. "I wanted to…" His voice trailed off, and he got a warning look from her.

"Remember, Brock, you promised not to lie. Omission is a lie."

His eyes shuttered in acknowledgment. "I wanted to control the outcome."

"Of the book."

"And…" He flicked a finger from her to him. "This."

"There isn't a *this*," she replied without a nanosecond of hesitation. "There was a *that* last night, but no *this* tonight."

He felt a smile tug at his lips. "You're good with words."

"Most of the time. Sometimes, I get the rug pulled out from under me." She leaned over the table. "And I get screwed."

He closed his eyes, hating that she might even think about putting him in that category. "I don't want to..." *Careful, Brock.* "See you fail." When she didn't answer, he added, "And, yes, I want to make sure that the Blackthorne family, businesses, and brand come out looking great."

"Just so we're clear," she said. "*Great* isn't always the point of a book like this. You realize that, don't you? This won't be a fawning fan book."

"What exactly are you looking for, then?"

"A number of things," she said. "Readers will want me to tear back the veneer on this family that someone has polished to a shine and make each and every one of you real, warts and all. They want...secrets."

He held up his hand to stop the assault. She wasn't getting any secrets. "Nothing that interesting. Not today, anyway. The family is just...normal."

She snorted and lifted her glass. "New drinking game. Take a sip every time Brock puts up a roadblock by telling me the Blackthornes are normal, boring, or just like every other family."

"We are," he insisted.

"Dysfunctional?"

"Not in the least," he countered, squashing down the memory of his aunt flying off to France. "With the minor exception that we have incredibly successful family-run businesses, we are just another large, blended family of brothers, cousins, aunts, uncles, and one feisty old nana who can drink us all under the table."

Her eyes flashed. "Can't wait to meet her."

"She's in Maine."

"Awesome. I can go up this weekend."

"I can't," he said.

"First of all, I don't need you. Second, didn't you say something about clearing your calendar, or was that…not true?"

He swallowed. "It's true, I just didn't know you meant weekends. Anyway, I have to go up later this month for the Founder's Day celebration, so we'll get you there eventually."

"Eventually?" She put her hand on his to drive home whatever she was about to say. "Brock, I have twenty-one days to get as many interviews as I can. I'm working weekends, nights, mornings, and anything else that's left. And I'd like to go wherever I can to see Blackthornes in action."

"That's Boston and Maine, mostly, though we have a big distillery in Kentucky, and my brother Jason is in LA running the entertainment end of the business."

"I'd like to see the estate in King Harbor," she said. "It's what people think of when they think about Blackthornes. King Harbor and whisky."

"We'll get there." Unless he could just run her around corporate for a few weeks and avoid any land mines.

"So, let's talk about it," she said, a slight sigh indicating she was willing to give up the push, at least for the moment. "Tell me all about this…" She gestured toward the glass. "Taste of tradition."

Finally, he was on solid, familiar, Blackthorne ground. No mention of Claire's leaving, thank God, which he would be sure to keep from Jenna.

And now he could talk about something that didn't make him think about...all the things he shouldn't be thinking about. Like how he could possibly be her "source" for all things Blackthorne and not want to kiss her as often as possible.

That was definitely going to be a challenge.

Chapter Six

Jenna's mother would say, "Let them talk. In between the lines, you'll find what you're looking for."

So Jenna let Brock talk. She peppered him with questions, but it didn't take many for him to shower her in Blackthorne history, delight her with his knowledge of distillery details, and basically draw out her attention, enthusiasm, and a lot of laughs that were still bubbling up as they walked out of the restaurant.

The only thing she found was a deep sense of attraction, a wistfulness that she couldn't kiss him again, and a charm that was as infectious as his smile. Nothing she could put into a book proposal.

"You know you're going to have to tell me all that again," she said. "I couldn't pull out a notebook at Menton."

"I'll tell you and so will half the other people you talk to."

Waiting for their car, Brock put a hand on her back and led her into the shadows on the sidewalk, his touch so warm and sure, it was easy to follow.

"I won't mind," she said. "I told you your family isn't boring. First of all, there are so many of them. For me, it was just Char, Sam, and Jenna tagging along."

"You call your parents by their first names?"

"I do," she said on a laugh. "I have no recollection of calling them Mommy and Daddy. I called them what they called each other, and they never corrected me." One of the many weirdnesses of her upbringing. "So, yes, I loved hearing all that, Brock. I can't wait to go back to my hotel and write it all up. I already know how I want to open the book."

"Tell me."

She shook her head. "Can't jinx it."

He searched her face for a long moment, sending the same warm rush through her that the whisky had. "So does that mean you want to get back to your hotel so you can burn the midnight oil? Because I know the Boston nightclub scene, or we could—"

"Oh, is that you, Brock?"

Jenna turned to see a couple step out of the restaurant behind them, a petite blonde and a much older man.

"Hello, Sarah," he said easily, accepting a friendly hug and a brush of her cheek.

"Do you know Gregg LaVigne of Northeast Liquor Stores?" The woman gestured toward her companion. "This is Brock Blackthorne."

"Oh?" the man responded, extending his hand for Brock to shake. "Never had the pleasure, Mr. Blackthorne."

"It's Brock, and this is Jenna Gillespie," he said. "Jenna, this gentleman is with one of our most valued retailers, and Sarah McKinney is part of McKinney Spirits Distribution, another customer."

"Maybe not a customer for long," Sarah said with a sly smile, which Jenna didn't understand.

But Brock angled his head, unfazed by the comment. "We'll see what happens," he said. "I've heard from my uncle that the acquisition discussions are going well."

"Well…enough," Sarah said.

"So, how's your father?" Brock asked. "Has he finished chemo?"

The other woman let out an understandable sigh. "Yes, but it's been rough. On my mother, too."

"I'm sure he and your uncle will be happy when our deal is done," Brock replied with plenty of sympathy in his tone, but the statement was met with a tight smile.

Jenna let her gaze shift from person to person, aware of a subtle volley going on and intrigued by it.

"Has your aunt Claire come back yet?" Sarah asked, raising a pointed eyebrow. "I heard she's been totally off the grid for months now. It was all so…stunning at her party."

Stunning?

Only because Jenna had been studying Brock all night and watching him relax as the evening wore on did she notice that his broad shoulders tensed and his jaw locked ever so slightly at the question. His aunt was "off the grid" for months? She'd never read or heard anything about that.

"Oh, right," Brock murmured. "You were at the estate that night."

What night? Jenna wondered, fighting the urge to step closer and pick up the cues and nuances that told her much more than people realized.

"Lots of people are wondering how things unfolded since Claire made her grand exit." Sarah put her hand on Brock's arm. "We wouldn't want anything to affect the negotiations with Blackthorne and the McKinney brothers," she said.

Once again, she sensed Brock subtly respond, but his expression stayed unreadable. "Claire's enjoying a summer in Europe," he said. "Certainly nothing that would affect the acquisition of your company."

"But she's without your uncle?" Sarah asked pointedly. "I don't think I've ever even seen a picture where those two weren't glued at the hip. My mother always talks about what a nice couple they are. Or…were."

Brock managed the most casual of shrugs, but his eyes took on that look Jenna had seen when she talked about Salmon Falls Distillery and an old possibly stolen recipe. She saw his Adam's apple rise and fall and a tiny vein in his temple pulse. The signs of something she might describe in her book as the look of Blackthorne pride.

"They certainly do have a great relationship," he agreed after the slightest hesitation. "But everyone deserves an extended vacation now and then."

"If that's all it is," Sarah said with just enough doubt to imply it wasn't all *she* thought it was. "After all, she did mention keeping a secret when she left."

"A secret?" The other man, Gregg, stepped forward without any of Jenna's finesse. His curiosity was obvious; Jenna's was burning but quiet.

"That's what she said," Sarah continued. "She told Graham she'd kept his secret long enough and marched right out of the Blackthorne Estate in King Harbor."

A long-kept secret? Like…a stolen recipe that made millions?

"Aunt Claire always has a flair for melodrama," Brock said quickly, glancing over his shoulder as Hoyt pulled up in the car. "Great to see you, Sarah. And to meet you, Gregg." He put a hand on Jenna's back and nodded to Hoyt, signaling him to stay in the car. Was that for a faster escape?

And why did he want to escape at all?

He had the back door open in a flash, guiding Jenna into the seat. "Give your father my best," he said to Sarah as he got in the back and pulled the door closed. "Take us straight to the Colonnade, Hoyt."

Oh. So much for that nightcap and dancing. Which was fine, but something had made Brock want to end this night…something named Sarah.

"So what was that all about?" she asked casually.

"We're negotiating to buy Sarah's family's business," he said. "She's just yanking my chain to up the price."

Really? Jenna waited a beat, smoothing her dress before asking, "What's your aunt doing in Europe?"

He cleared his throat as if that might help him don an expression that told her nothing. "Like I said, having a fun summer, in Paris. And Sarah McKinney loves to have gossip to throw around with the wholesalers and customers. It makes her sound very plugged in."

"She didn't seem like a gossip," she mused, glancing out the window. "I take it her father has cancer?"

"And his brother's ready to retire to Hawaii, making McKinney a hot commodity for us."

But there was so much more than that. "She seemed unhappy that your aunt is out of the country."

"We all are," he said with a flicker in his eyes that could be interpreted only as regret for having said a word.

"Why?"

He took a slow inhale and blew it out. "It's a boring story."

"Take a drink," she joked, making him smile. After a second, she leaned a little closer. "There's nothing boring about a secret," she whispered. "I'm kind of building my whole career on them."

He slid her a glance. "Is that really what you want? Secrets and lies?"

"Not lies," she shot back. "Please, for heaven's sake, no lies."

His expression softened as he held her gaze for two full heartbeats. "Then don't go after idle gossip, which is nothing you'd want to include in a book as factual and accurate as yours."

"You sure seem to care about it."

"I care about anything that affects the Blackthorne brand."

"Idle gossip?"

"Can wreck acquisition deals," he told her.

That made sense...sort of. "And the secret?"

He snorted. "Sarah is reading too much into that night."

"What happened?"

He shifted in his seat and turned to look out the window, silent, which only made Jenna want to know more.

She added a little pressure to his shoulder with hers. "Hey."

He turned, brows raised. "Hey?"

"I'd say hey to David." She narrowed her eyes at him. "And I thought you weren't lying anymore... David." She whispered the last word so only he could hear it.

For a long moment, he said nothing, searching her face, lingering over her mouth long enough to make her feel a natural and feminine response.

"Should I put my glasses on?" he asked with a hopeful tease.

"Not going to lie. I thought they were kinda sexy." Then she smiled. "Which takes nerve coming from a woman who looked like a drowned mongoose when we met."

"Obviously, I thought that mongoose was hot."

A slow smile pulled at her lips. "And got hotter as the night went on."

He gave a slight grunt. "I'm trying to forget."

"Yeah, me, too," she admitted.

"It's not easy."

"So not easy." She laughed and turned to face him. "Sometimes, I catch a glimmer of…David, and I'm…" *Hungry for more.* "Sad he's gone."

"He's not gone."

The words, whispered right into her ear, sent chills through her and started a familiar burn low in her belly. She shouldn't do this, and she knew it. But holding his gaze, touching his arm, losing herself in the look in his eyes…it was all too tempting.

He hesitated a moment, then leaned to his left, touched the armrest, and a dark privacy panel rose between them and the driver. The move was slick, subtle, and downright sexy.

She tried to swallow, but her throat was tight. If he kissed her…could she possibly stop, get out of this limo, and send him away?

He held his finger up as if asking her to wait and touched one of his eyes, then the other. "Disposables," he said, rubbing his fingers on a handkerchief he produced.

"Did you just take your contacts out?" she asked on a soft, surprised laugh.

"Yep. And now this." He reached to his tie knot, loosened it, then slowly and deliberately pulled the silky fabric until it opened. Every second, her mouth grew drier and her heart beat faster.

He slid the tie off completely, then, still holding her gaze and giving her the slightest smile, he reached into the jacket that lay next to him, pulled out the same glasses he wore last night, and put them on.

"Clark Kent is back," she whispered, her voice hoarse and tight.

"You can call me David." He put his hand on her cheek, stroking it with a touch that somehow managed to be hot and feather-light. "The man you ride in cars with. The man you run in the rain with. The man you..." He came a little closer, near enough that she could feel his breath and had to close her eyes to handle the impact. "Kiss."

She tilted her head so his lips landed exactly where she wanted them on her mouth, sucking in a soft breath at the shock of just how good it felt. He kept the kiss light, maddeningly so, more of a brush of lips than the dozens of kisses they'd shared last night.

But when she groaned at the sheer pleasure of his mouth, he slid his hand under her hair and eased her closer, adding pressure and warmth and the sweet tip of his tongue.

Jenna closed her eyes and shut out all the many thoughts that said it was wrong, stupid, foolish, and dangerous to kiss the man who could make or break this book for her. Instead, she just listened to the hum of blood in her head, the sound of their heartbeats, and the sigh that he let out when they parted.

"David," she whispered, reaching up to take those glasses off for the next kiss. "I kissed David, not Brock." She slid the glasses into his unbuttoned shirt and leaned in for another kiss.

He laughed. "I can bring him out to play anytime you want." He opened his mouth a little, and she did the same, both of them shuddering as a now familiar burn flickered into a fire in her body.

"I'll walk you up," he whispered as the car came to a stop.

Bad idea. So bad.

"Okay, but tell your driver to wait for you," she replied. "I have to turn all that Blackthorne history into notes tonight."

"Of course," he said, but the glint of disappointment was easy to read.

"You know anything else would be crazy," she said.

"Insane," he agreed.

"Ruinous."

He laughed. "An absolute tragedy."

"It would be…"

He kissed her lightly as he tapped on the window for Hoyt to get the door. "Just the worst night ever. *Again.*"

Still smiling at the exchange, they climbed out as the driver waited, and Brock walked her into the empty lobby and to the elevator. There, he put on his glasses, a mix of dark rims and wire frames.

"Never thought these things would get me a girl."

She tapped his chest. "You didn't get her tonight."

When the doors opened, she stepped inside and held up one hand to keep him out. He gave a simple nod, but she saw the heat in his eyes and the promise and longing and lust he didn't bother to hide.

Then the doors closed, and she fell back against the wall.

Stupid. Crazy. Insane. Dangerous. Foolish. Ruinous. Tragic.

Yeah, it would be all those things.

And so damn *good*.

It wasn't until Jenna reached her hotel room and put

63

the key in the door that she realized that Brock Blackthorne had just used the oldest form of distraction known to man. What better way to stop her line of questioning than…that? But, oh wow. What a way to go.

If she could make it through the next three weeks without getting in bed with him again, it would be as much of a miracle as if she sold this proposal.

She knew which of those two things she needed more. And she had to remember that.

Chapter Seven

S he could get used to this.

Jenna stepped into the summer sunshine the next morning and caught the eye of Brock's driver outside of the hotel, waiting next to an understated black town car.

"Ms. Gillespie," he said with a nod, instantly moving to open the back door. "How are you this morning?"

She gave him her brightest smile to cover that she was exhausted from a night of writing and research that ended at three in the morning. "I'm wonderful, Hoyt. Or is it Mr. Hoyt?" She angled her head and gave the silver-haired man a smile. "I don't know anything about you."

His eyes flickered with surprise as he gestured for her to get in the car. "Hoyt Ashgrove, ma'am, and there is not much to know."

So Blackthornes trained their employees to answer that way, too. "I don't believe that's true about anyone," she said as she situated herself in the back seat. "I bet, by the time we get to Blackthorne Enterprises, I'll know your secret."

"Don't have one," he said on a chuckle. "Plus, it's only a mile or so, ma'am. And I know how to avoid traffic."

"Plenty of time," she said, unfazed.

She had her first question ready by the time he climbed in behind the steering wheel. "Do you have kids, Hoyt?"

"Our son, Sean, is deployed in Afghanistan right now, and so is his wife." She could hear the pride in his voice and noticed that when he said it, he reached forward and touched the dashboard. When his hand moved, she could see he'd grazed his finger over a piece of white paper with tiny writing.

"That must be difficult for you."

"Oh, they'll be fine. Marines, both of them, and tough as nails." His voice trailed off as he turned into traffic, and maybe realized his job wasn't to chat up the Blackthorne guests when he drove them. But he hadn't driven Jenna Gillespie alone yet.

"Have you worked for the Blackthornes very long?" she asked, keeping her questions as light and conversational as possible, just like her mother taught her as a way to open up a subject.

"Almost a decade," he said. "I've had many jobs with the company, too. I drove the senior Mr. Blackthorne for several years and now work primarily for Brock and fill in as a driver for some of the others in the family."

She inched forward with interest. "Have you driven Mrs. Blackthorne?" Maybe he could shed some light on what happened with Claire, because that was one aspect of this family she hadn't found in any article, interview, or marketing material she'd been through until the wee hours.

"Yes, I have," he said with a smile. "Mrs. B has been so good to my little granddaughter."

Oh. He had a young granddaughter? And his son and daughter-in-law were both deployed? She squinted at the small piece of paper he'd touched, not able to read it, but she could see from the tiny numbers with a colon between them that it must be a Bible quote.

"When little Janie turned four last fall, Mrs. B made sure we had the most amazing birthday party for her," he continued. "Clowns, balloons, one of those big bouncy houses."

"How sweet." So Claire was thoughtful, family-oriented, and generous. And in Europe.

"It took the sting out of her parents not being here, you know." She heard the pain in the words and imagined just how difficult it was for this family.

"Are you taking care of Janie while her parents are deployed?" she asked.

"Oh yeah. Never thought I'd be tripping over toys and dolls at sixty-eight, but there you have it." He chuckled and crossed the intersection, slowing down in front of the Hancock Tower. "I'm available all day, Ms. Gillespie, if you need a driver. Just talk to Karen, Brock's assistant."

"I will, Hoyt, thank you." She gathered her bag as he parked, waiting for him to climb out and open the door for her.

"I told you I was rather uninteresting," he said as she stepped out.

"A man who spoils his granddaughter with toys, prays for her parents every day, and has postponed retirement to make sure he can provide for her no matter what?"

His jaw loosened.

"I'd say you're quite interesting, Hoyt."

"But you didn't get any secret," he said with a smile. "Raising my granddaughter and praying for her is no secret. I'm proud of both."

"I bet you are. And I'm so pleased to hear the Blackthornes are so supportive. I'll be sure to work that into the book I'm writing."

He nodded. "Mr. Blackthorne told me you were writing a tell-all."

She couldn't help curling her lip at the expression. "I prefer to think of it as an in-depth study of a fascinating family."

"They are that," he agreed.

"Who do you think is the best person to interview?" she asked as they walked toward the building, comfortable that the short ride had developed a good rapport. "The senior Mr. Blackthorne?"

He snorted. "Good luck getting time with him."

"Brock's admin?" The support staff always knew good stuff.

"She'll never say a thing that Brock wouldn't." He glanced from side to side. "You want to talk to Mrs. B, but…" His expression fell.

"Do you think she'll be coming back soon?"

On a sigh, he pulled the heavy glass door. "I sure hope so," he said quietly. "Janie keeps asking about her."

It seemed like everyone felt the absence of this great lady. Why would she take off from her birthday party and leave so many people missing her? Jenna tucked the question away and ended the conversation with a bright smile.

"Shopkins," she said to him.

"Excuse me?"

"Next time you're at a drugstore, ask if they have Shopkins. Janie will love them."

He frowned. "New one on me."

She remembered the interview she'd done with Susannah Villeneuve while her little girl had played in a mountain of toys, interrupting constantly to show Jenna the miniature dollhouse items. "It's my pro tip for you."

He grinned. "Shopkins. Good to know, Ms. Gillespie."

"Now I better go. I'm already late, and I have a feeling Brock won't like that at all."

"No, he doesn't do late." As he held the door to the Hancock Tower lobby, he dipped his head and narrowed his eyes a bit. "So here's *my* pro tip. If you go around the bank of elevators to the right, take a short hall and look for the sign that says Private Express, that elevator only goes to executive levels in the building. Take it to the fifty-third floor, and you'll go straight to Blackthorne's mahogany row. You just have to key in 1108, which is the Blackthorne family code."

She pointed playfully. "See? I got a secret from you after all."

He laughed. "Well, I guess you did. But that number's not that tough to figure out, since it has to be something everyone in the family can remember."

"Eleven-o-eight?" she asked, trying to guess what it was.

"Mr. and Mrs. Blackthorne's wedding anniversary."

"Good to know, and thank you, sir." She gave a little formal bow, which he returned, along with that sparkle in his eye, giving her the confidence—and insider info—to head straight to the executive express elevator.

There, a handsome older man stood waiting for the elevator, looking down at a picture on his phone. She stole the quickest glance, catching the image of a woman with long, silver hair, but stayed a few feet away so as not to be rude. And then she took a closer look at the man and sucked in a little breath of recognition, making him instantly turn to her.

"Graham Blackthorne?" she asked, since it was obvious she'd recognized him.

He lifted his brows, which were darker than his salt-and-pepper hair, interest glinting in dark eyes that reminded her very much of Brock. His jaw was still defined, despite his sixty years, and he had broad shoulders and an imposing air that oozed power and wealth.

"I'm Jenna Gillespie." She reached out her hand to shake his. "Working on a project with your nephew Brock."

"Ad agency?" he guessed, giving her a cursory, but strong handshake.

"No, no, I'm in publishing."

The doors opened, and he let her go first, then crossed his arms and looked toward the keypad, as if daring her to know the secret code. She probably wasn't supposed to be in here, but she sure didn't want to miss this chance.

Without Brock to steer and guide the conversation, this moment was interview gold. And Brock would no doubt be furious not to be next to her when she talked to a Blackthorne, but right now, opportunity knocked. Well, it presented a keypad, which she touched with one confident index finger.

"One-one-oh-eight," she said brightly as she keyed in the numbers.

He kept a keen gaze on her. "What was it you said you're doing with Brock?"

"I didn't say." She reached into the side of her bag and pulled out a card she kept handy. "I'm writing a book about your family, Mr. Blackthorne."

"A book?" A frown furrowed his brow as he read her card. "I know nothing about this."

"I'm pretty sure you will today. I have a series of meetings with family members, and I hope Brock has you on that list."

"Oh, wait, yes. I forgot." His gaze dropped over her, a quick assessment, a moment to think, and then he nodded, sliding the card into his suit jacket pocket. "Ollie Hazlett mentioned this to me when we golfed a few weeks ago."

Her stomach dropped a little, and not just because the car started its climb up fifty-three floors. How much had Ollie Hazlett told him?

"He's my publisher," she confirmed, hoping Hazlett wasn't so stupid that he'd tell Graham Blackthorne that Jenna's last project had been killed while the book was actually being printed. "Would you be able to find a few minutes to talk to me, Mr. Blackthorne?"

"Depends on what you want to talk about."

"You," she said simply.

He huffed a quick breath. "Don't expect family dirt from me."

"I don't want dirt," she assured him. "I want to know one thing."

Expressionless, he waited to hear what it was.

"I mean, I want to know a lot of things, like history and big events and turning points for the Blackthorne family and company, but from you, just one thing." She inched closer and held his gaze, channeling her inner Charlotte May.

"Yes?" he asked.

"What is the single moment in your life that gave you the most joy?"

He stared at her, still no smile, but she sensed the wheels spinning in those dark and foreboding eyes. "Joy?" The worded sounded gruff on his lips.

She nodded, hoping that the question, which she'd heard her mother ask many times on television, would be the catalyst for something he really wanted to talk about, enough that he'd guide her right into his office for a cup of coffee and a real interview.

Joy was the secret to get people talking, she'd heard her mother say. Joy was family, security, home, hearth, and holidays. Joy was a great door opener, much better than regrets or do-overs or legacies.

"Joy," he said one more time, his voice a little wistful that time. He shifted his gaze from her face to the keypad, staring at it for a long time. Long enough that chills rose on her arms, and her throat grew tight. Finally, just as the car came to a stop, he pointed at the pad where she'd typed in his anniversary date. "That," he said softly. "That was pure joy."

Obviously, he didn't mean the moment she'd used the keypad.

"Would you tell me about it?"

"No." The doors opened, and he stepped out without offering her to exit first, disappearing around the corner without so much as a goodbye.

What was going on with Graham and Claire?

Something was very wrong in Blackthorne Land, and if she could figure out what it was, there was no way she'd lose this book deal.

Chapter Eight

B rock looked at his watch and frowned, surprised that Jenna would be even one minute late. Had the kiss been…too much?

No. That kiss was *not enough*. And they both knew it.

He should have known the minute the idea occurred to him that the cliché distraction would have a bigger benefit than just stopping the questions about Claire. He should have known that the very minute he kissed her again, they'd both want to go flying back to the night before when they'd been strangers…and lovers.

Good idea? Guess it depended on who was asking. It sure felt right to him, but he obviously had the power in this relationship. For that reason, if nothing else, anything that happened between them would have to be her call. But this morning, he was tense, waiting to see her.

Walking out of his office to Karen's desk, he looked around and down the hall toward reception, surprised at the thud of disappointment when he didn't see Jenna's bright blue eyes and blond hair. Maybe she got lost. Maybe she got detoured. Maybe she was on another floor digging up whatever she could find on his family.

"Has she checked in downstairs yet?" he asked Karen when she turned from a filing cabinet.

"Oh, Hoyt just texted that she's in the private express elevator."

He drew back at that. "I didn't give her the code. Did you?"

"Nope."

Then Hoyt must have, which was a testament to just how much that woman could worm out of people. Even people he'd trust with his life, like Hoyt Ashgrove. Yeah, he better—

"I need you, *stat*." Trey whipped around the corner into Brock's office area with an expression that was more serious than usual. His dark eyes were tapered to concerned slits, his voice tense with control. No matter what had his cousin and the oldest Blackthorne riled this morning, it had not, of course, taken one business-short hair out of place or made him so much as loosen the Windsor knot at his throat.

But Brock would expect nothing else from the man long ago anointed to take over the reins of Blackthorne Enterprises.

"What's going on?" Brock asked, momentarily forgetting Jenna and the meetings he'd lined up with her today.

"Riverfront just canceled their most recent PO, and the rep says they have no plans to open another one," Trey said.

Brock processed everything about that cryptic news, instantly recognizing why it rose to the level of a fire that had to be extinguished immediately. Riverfront Liquor was the largest chain retail store in the Midwest and a big Blackthorne customer. A critical loss, but something like that didn't usually concern Brock. "And this involves brand management how?"

"The rep said something about 'company issues' and

concerns that the spirits division might not be under the 'best management' at the moment." Along with air quotes, he added a look that spoke volumes, and instantly Brock understood. Karen must have, too, since she immediately stood and stepped into Brock's office to leave the two men alone.

Management of the largest and most wildly profitable division in the company would mean Graham, his uncle and Trey's father. Doubts would mean...Claire. Oh yeah, the rumor mill was in overdrive in the liquor industry since his aunt had taken off. The brand was most definitely in jeopardy.

"Okay," Brock said, glancing in the direction of the express elevator. "I have a meeting about to—"

"Reschedule." Trey pointed to his office with just enough demand in his voice to remind Brock that not only was the man his cousin, he was his boss. "We'll get the rep on the line and fly out to Chicago if we have to."

Chicago? This week? Of course, Trey would put life, family, and his next breath second to a corporate crisis. And Brock wouldn't normally argue, but something just as pressing was on his agenda, and she had yet to show up this morning.

"Are you sure I need to be there?"

Trey's dark brows shot up. "The brand is on the line with a major customer." He sounded a little disappointed, or maybe surprised, that he'd even have to remind Brock of that. "See you in two minutes. I'm going to get my dad."

Just as Trey disappeared around the corner, Brock heard a woman clear her throat behind him, making him turn to see Jenna. How much of that had she heard?

"Something wrong?" she asked.

He took a moment before answering, taking in the impact of her fair hair spilling over a navy-blue dress that was businesslike enough to blend in, but something about the crisp white collar managed to look sexy, too.

Damn it, Trey. Chicago? This week?

Except…he should want to leave town. Work was way more important than some silly tell-all biography, no matter how pretty the package that came with it. Fact was, he should be relieved to go take care of business and send Jenna off with a good excuse. Trey's lost purchase order was a gift, and he should take it. Not stand here and…imagine that dress on the bedroom floor the same way he'd flung off that little yellow T-shirt thing she'd worn.

And under it…

"I'm very sorry," he said, mentally punching back the image. "We just had a crisis arise, and I don't know how long I'm going to be out of pocket."

"Oh, that's fine." She flicked her hand, not remotely fazed by this curve ball. "I'll just poke around, talk to people, make friends." She added a reassuring smile. "I'm fine on my own, Brock."

Oh, no, she wasn't. "Well, my admin can—"

"Help you with anything you need," Karen said, breezing back to her desk. "I have her schedule, Brock, and I'm happy to escort Ms. Gillespie to the meetings you've arranged, except the first one doesn't start for an hour."

"I planned to take her on a tour."

"Of offices?" Karen shot him a look, because, really, a tour of corporate cubes was pretty damn dull. "You deal with Trey, Mr. Blackthorne. I'll escort your guest."

But his guest didn't need an escort. She needed someone to rein in talkative people and put the right spin on everything she heard. With her keen questions and innocent-sounding prodding, she'd have more information about this company, his family, and God knows what than if she were plying the staff with Blackthorne Gold.

"No," he said simply. "Jenna can wait for me."

Jenna choked a soft laugh. "You think I should just sit in your office like a prisoner?"

"Why don't I take Jenna down to see Logan?" Karen interjected, giving Brock a glance that said she understood his concerns and that Logan could be trusted.

Sure, his cousin could be trusted to talk the Blackthorne talk and walk the Blackthorne walk. But one look at Jenna, and Logan would whip out his famous charm and humor and…then Logan would be the one imagining her dress on the floor.

"I didn't realize Logan was here," he said, but then, the youngest of all the Blackthorne brothers and cousins had the kind of schedule—and job—that made it difficult to keep track of the man.

"He's working with some of the product development team on a potential new product aimed at women. Jenna would be welcome in that meeting, I think."

"Oooh." Jenna stepped forward, blinding him with a smile. "Product development. That sounds interesting."

No doubt she'd be asking about ancient myths and stolen recipes. "You can't sit in on product development. It's top secret."

Her eyes widened like he'd just waved steak in front of a dog. "I'll sign a nondisclosure for product stuff. I'd love to soak up the process, not the latest announcement about chocolate salted bourbon, or whatever you're dreaming up for women." She held up two fingers. "Scout's honor."

He considered that for a moment, studying her pretty face and silently cursing Trey again. He was the damn CEO-to-be, not Brock. Trey should be going to the mat with Riverfront.

"You don't have to sign anything," he finally said. "I trust you."

Jenna angled her head and slayed him with those baby blues. "Thank you, Mr. Blackthorne."

"After all," he added, "I get to preview and approve anything you write."

All the sweetness disappeared, and her jaw dropped so hard and fast, he could have sworn he'd heard it crack. "What?"

"Any day, Brock!"

At the sound of Trey's impatient call, Jenna gave him a nudge. "Crisis calls," she said. "You go. I'll hit the product development meeting, and we'll discuss that preview thing later."

Wait a second. Who was calling the shots around here? "This won't take long," he said, but even as he promised that, he knew it could take hours.

Karen put a hand on Jenna's shoulder. "Product development is down a floor. Come with me."

Even though Trey called one more time, Brock stayed right where he was and watched Jenna walk away, knowing in his gut that Blackthorne Enterprises was chock-full of people who loved to gossip, spread rumors, and ply outsiders with inside information. This really was the worst place for her to be.

Down in product development, she'd be surrounded by loose lips and new faces eager to chat up the company biographer.

And just forget the fact that she'd be spending time with Logan. From the time Brock had moved into the

Blackthorne house in Weston at nine years old, he and Logan, as the youngest of both families, had shared a bedroom. Brock knew his cousin's secret weapon was humor. And brains. And that boyish charm that could melt the pants off…most women. And frequently did.

As he walked toward Trey's office, Brock made a quick and easy decision. Screw Chicago. Trey was the one in line for the most coveted job in the company, not Brock. Hell, as the youngest nephew, not a son of the CEO, Brock was the very last of the seven Blackthorne men who'd ever get that honor, no matter how much he secretly yearned for the job.

He'd help Trey and Graham with the damage control, then he wanted Jenna to think she was learning everything about the Blackthornes but really see only the best side of the whole family.

There was only one way to do that. He had to get her out of here and to a place where he could keep her by his side every minute of every day. And, maybe, night.

Jenna didn't know which hurt more after two hours in Logan Blackthorne's hilarious and brilliant meeting. Her cheeks from laughing, or her hand from writing notes. Not only did the man seem to know everything about every aspect of a massive business, he had his finger on the pulse of the culture, millennials, and the bar scene they were selling their product to.

As the room emptied, she rubbed the knuckles of her right hand with her left, shaking her fingers to ease them while she watched Logan finish up a one-on-one conversation with the distillery operations manager, who'd spent much of the meeting helping the team understand what could and couldn't be done with whisky.

But her gaze stayed on Logan, who was as easy on the eyes as the other Blackthornes she'd met, and just as fascinating. Like Brock, and even Trey and Graham, though her encounters with them had been brief, the men in this family seemed to have an underlying grit and steel that blended with that constant hum of pride and confidence in everything they did.

"You should try this new invention called a laptop." Logan sauntered toward Jenna after the other man left. She'd taken a seat on the side of the room, not that staying away from the conference table had kept her from answering the "outsider" questions the group of five professionals had thrown at her during the meeting. "It really beats the old stone and chisel." He gestured toward her notebook and winked.

"I'm old-fashioned that way." She capped her pen, but purposely left her notebook open in case this one-on-one revealed anything worth nothing.

"Not so old-fashioned you don't understand what young women like to drink."

She smiled at him. "You sure understand it."

He laughed easily, dropping into the chair next to her. "Did it sound like I know my way around the bar scene just a little too well for a man eight years out of college?"

"You sounded like a man who knows his way around a product that is all about fun and the women he's trying to get to buy it."

His dark eyes sparked as he leaned a little closer to whisper, "Don't tell Brock. He sees the brand as all about 'taste, tradition, and two hundred years of Blackthorne pride.'"

"He has a deep and abiding respect for the Blackthorne brand," she said, not quite sure why she felt she had to defend Brock, but she did.

"It's more than that," he told her. "With Brock, *everything* is about the brand, the business, and the image portrayed by that damn barrel-and-thistle logo he likes to slap on everything from bottle labels to cocktail napkins in the tasting bar, whether they need it or not."

Intrigued to learn anything about Brock, she inched closer. "You think that's what's most important to him? In life?"

He thought about the question for a moment, then lifted an impressive shoulder and slipped into a smile that seemed to be very much a part of who this casual, easygoing man was.

"His respect for the brand is more like..." He trailed off with one more shrug, but Jenna put her hand on his arm to ever so gently prod more out of him.

"Like?"

But she saw a sudden protectiveness in his eyes. "Let him tell you his story, Jenna."

"He has a story?"

He angled his head, seeming surprised she didn't know. "Brock, Jason, and Phillip are our cousins. You know that, don't you?"

"Yes, of course."

"And they lived with us since my aunt Julie and my uncle Mark died in a plane crash twenty years or so ago. Brock was nine."

She nodded, aware of this history, but not any of the details. He'd carefully kept their conversation last night focused on business not family, and nothing about his own childhood. That would have been too personal, and personal would lead to...intimate. But she so wanted to know more—both for the book and for her own interest in Brock.

"And you think that childhood history is why he's so protective of the brand?" she asked.

"Of the family. Of the name. His brothers are older, and they have their own issues where their parents' deaths are concerned. But Brock has always been...grateful." He was quiet for a moment, then shook his head as if he'd made a mental decision. "Let Brock tell you."

"Let Brock tell you what?"

She turned at the sound of Brock's voice and saw him standing in the conference room doorway, looking imposing and maybe not thrilled with his cousin at that moment.

Instantly, Logan stood. "Hey, man. How are you?" He walked over and gave Brock an easy handshake and brotherly pat on the back. "How the hell can I thank you for this wonderful gift?" He gestured toward Jenna, impressing her with his ease at shifting the conversation from serious to light.

"Gift?" Brock asked.

"I know Jenna was supposed to be scooping up intel for this book she's writing, but I'm afraid I didn't give her much."

Brock gave him a dubious look, making Jenna wonder just how much of her conversation with Logan he'd heard.

"But we didn't have a woman in the room under fifty, and I needed to hear from another millennial. When our version of skinny bourbon hits the bars next year, we can thank Jenna for the label idea."

"The label?"

"Don't worry, King of Branding. You'll get final approval before we even start testing the focus groups.

In fact, I'm going up to marketing now to get some ideas rolling." He turned to Jenna and threw her another easy smile. "Great to talk to you, Jenna. Good luck with the book. I know you're in good hands with this guy here."

With a casual salute, he slipped out of the conference room, leaving them alone.

"How goes the crisis?" Jenna asked, closing her notebook and standing.

"It's solved for the moment." He took a few steps closer, searching her face as if looking for something there. "Did you get anything out of this meeting other than charmed by my cousin?"

"He is charming," she agreed. "And I learned a lot about what goes into creating a new line of whisky. But…" She let out a sigh. "That's not really a big part of what I want to write."

"You're worried about that proposal."

"The clock's ticking," she agreed. "I really hope I can spend some time with your family and long-term employees, rather than being mired in corporate stuff. I need to get to the heart and soul of this family, or I'm going to fail."

"I know that, so let's get you back to the hotel to pack."

Seriously? "I'm not ready to leave yet. I haven't even started."

"That's why we're leaving."

Now she was totally confused. "To go where?"

"King Harbor, Maine." He put a hand on her shoulder, leading her toward the door. "You wanted to visit it, right?"

"Yes, but—"

"The Blackthorne Estate *is* the heart and soul of the family. We can drive up there, grab lunch in a little place on the coast I love, and have time to see the sunset."

She eyed him, considering this new twist and what it could mean to her writing and information gathering. "As lovely as that sounds, I'm not really on a mission to have lunch and see sunsets."

"You just said you don't want to be mired in the corporate stuff."

"I want to talk to the people who make up the family."

"Exactly. There's plenty of family in Maine, including my nana, who knows and, with enough to drink, tells."

"That sounds...promising."

He laughed and added a little pressure to steer her down the hall toward the elevator. "You go to the hotel to pack, and I'll go home, do the same, and pick you up in an hour. Wear a jacket. It can get windy with the top down."

"Hoyt has a convertible in that fleet?"

He laughed. "I'm driving, Jenna. We'll get there faster, windblown and happy." He inched closer to whisper in her ear, "Added benefit, I'm way more David than I am Brock up there."

She tried to shoot him a warning look, but his smile was downright devastating, so she just had to laugh. "All right, *David*. Let's go to Maine."

Chapter Nine

He hadn't been kidding about David, Brock realized as they got farther from town and traffic. He'd always known that when he saw Boston in the rearview mirror and headed north toward Maine that a switch clicked in him that took the edge away, but he'd never really noticed how marked a difference it was.

With the wind in his hair, the sun beating down, and the smell of sea salt heralding "home," Brock was more than content with the decision to leave Boston. He and Jenna didn't talk much over the roar of the Porsche 911 motor, but the silence was comfortable, and his passenger seemed as relaxed as he was. The magic of Maine, he thought, the moment they left New Hampshire and reached the outskirts of Kittery. That would mean…food.

"We have to stop for lobster rolls," he announced, leaning close so Jenna could hear him and also because she smelled good. "And ice cream."

She laughed, brushing back a strand of blond hair and tucking it behind her ear. "I thought we were going to King Harbor to research my book."

"This is research. Lobster rolls at McMathers and ice cream at The Crazy Cow are in our family DNA. You can't know how the Blackthornes lived until you've been to all our hangouts. And tonight, in King Harbor, we'll drink at The Whisky Vault, or the Vault, as locals and family call it."

"More research?" she asked on a laugh.

"The best kind. Seriously, you can't drive up to King Harbor and not stop at these landmarks, Jenna," he told her as he pulled off at the next exit. "It's Blackthorne tradition."

He drove a few familiar miles down a windy, thickly wooded road until the brush opened up to reveal a small lake and two ramshackle buildings that served some of the best food on the East Coast. No surprise, the small parking lot had at least two dozen cars, and many of the picnic tables were full.

McMathers was no more than a one-window, gray, weathered shack with a faded sign that had to be from the sixties, owned by a family known for making the best lobster rolls on earth. About fifty yards away, on the other side of a grassy area, stood the white clapboard ice cream store called The Crazy Cow.

As they climbed out of his car, Jenna slipped out of the denim jacket she'd been wearing, looking from one notorious place of business to the other. "Somehow, this is not how I imagined Blackthornes eat." She shook her hair out of a ponytail into a wild blond mane, her eyes bright from the ride.

"My aunt Claire discovered this place when I was really young." He took a slow breath, letting his gaze travel what, for Brock, was hallowed grounds full of memories. Not all happy, but they were solid, and they made him who he was. "We used to all come up together, my mom and dad with Phillip and Jason and me in one car, and our cousins with Uncle Graham and Aunt Claire in the other, always in tandem for some reason I'll never understand. Of course, someone was always hungry or had to go to the bathroom, so we'd stop here. After a few years, it became tradition."

He ushered her toward McMathers, slipping further back in time with each step.

"That tradition didn't change after your parents died?" she asked, her voice gentle enough for him to know she realized she was treading on sensitive ground.

He smiled to assure her that the topic was fine and that time had made it easy for him to talk about Julie and Mark Blackthorne. "In some ways, everything changed, but my aunt and uncle made sure that, in other ways, nothing changed."

They reached the window, and she let him order their lobster rolls and drinks, which were served on paper plates and in plastic cups that they took to one of the picnic tables bathed in sunshine.

"Too bad the tables were replaced in the last ten years," he said as they sat down across from each other. "One of them had all our names carved with a knife my brother Phillip got grounded for carrying." He shook his head and laughed at the memory.

She picked up her lobster roll, but set it back down in a move he was beginning to recognize was a prelude to a question. Her questions always took precedence over food, drink, or any other distraction. He knew what was coming, though, and how long it would take to answer, so he took a few bites of the sweet chunks of lobster and buttery bread.

"Logan said you have a story, and I think he was talking about your parents' deaths. You were really young. I can only imagine how that affects a child."

Yep, she'd want to know that. He took a few minutes to chew and wipe his mouth with the rough paper napkin, then sipped the lemonade that was as much a part of this meal as the sandwich and sunshine.

"I was nine," he finally said. "My parents got into a private plane one afternoon to get Phillip who, no surprise to anyone, was in trouble at a sleep-away camp for a prank he'd pulled. My dad was a great pilot, instrument-rated, but they hit a storm that blew in out of nowhere and…" Now, this, he didn't like to talk about. The worst part of his parents' deaths was imagining what those last few minutes must have been like.

Her face reflected that she was thinking the same thing. "Storms," she murmured. "I hate them."

"We think the plane was hit by lightning, and my dad lost control."

"Oh my God."

He just nodded and covered any emotion with a deep drink of lemonade, but this time it didn't taste like summer and sunshine. It tasted bitter, like that summer that started with two parents and ended with a whole new normal.

Jenna reached across the picnic table to put her hand over his. "I'm so sorry for you. That's heartbreaking."

He let his gaze settle on her fingers and the comfort they offered. "It's been twenty years," he said. "Of course, not a day goes by that I don't wonder what life would have been like if they'd lived. And I'm a little ashamed that my memories are not much more than snapshots and wisps of moments that I can barely hold on to. But I can tell you this, I didn't ever feel like I was an orphan, and that was thanks to Claire and Graham and my four cousins. In any other family, that would have been a tragedy that the three of us might never have recovered from, but being a Blackthorne…"

Being a Blackthorne was what had saved him from being lost and alone.

"There was no question you and your brothers would live with your aunt and uncle? Your grandparents didn't have a say?"

"My parents left a very clear will and the whole transition was…seamless." Dark, scary, and definitely the worst summer of his life, but it could have been so much worse. "We were up in King Harbor when it happened, and in the summers, everyone lived at the estate. Even my dad and uncle, though they'd go down to Boston to work during the week. But the seven of us and my mom and Aunt Claire were up there from Memorial Day to Labor Day. So it wasn't like we were alone."

She nodded, listening with her whole body leaning closer. Her gaze was intent, her attention sharp. For the book? Or was this just an intimate conversation between two people who'd already been as intimate as possible? He didn't know. And right then, he didn't care. He wanted to tell her.

"When September rolled around that year, my brothers and I moved into the big Weston house like…" He shook his head so she wouldn't misunderstand him. "Obviously not like nothing ever happened, but I never lived a day thinking I didn't have a family. I missed my mom and dad, God, yes. But my aunt overcompensated and really made all three of us feel like we were her sons, too. Come Halloween, she sewed my costume. She went to our sporting events and cheered like a mom. She and my uncle wrapped their arms around us literally and figuratively. We already all went to the same private school, so life just went on, mostly thanks to Claire Blackthorne."

She'd taken a few bites while he talked, but she set her sandwich down again and leaned a little closer. "Have you talked to her since she left?"

"And here I thought you were digging through *my* emotional land mines, not looking for family secrets."

"So there *is* a secret?"

God, he had to remember who he was talking to. Trust and confidential revelations were huge risks he couldn't take. "Listen, Jenna, my aunt was just blowing off steam when she said that," he told her.

"But she was mad when she left?"

He shrugged. "It was her sixtieth birthday, so she was probably a little melancholy or having some kind of crisis about getting older. And she felt ignored by a husband who puts work above all else, since my uncle turned what was supposed to be a birthday party into a work event. So she got ticked off and took off. I don't think it means she's not coming back." At least, he hoped it didn't.

She searched his face. "Who said anything about her not coming back?"

Every word had to be watched with her. "No one." But they had passed the two-month mark, which Jenna would probably figure out just by researching Claire Blackthorne's birthday. "I just don't want you to think that's what's going on. That she and Graham aren't...fine."

"Are they?"

"Of course."

"Because when I talked to him, he—"

"You *talked* to him?" How could he not know that?

"In the express elevator. Hoyt gave me the code, but please don't be mad at—"

"What did you talk to him about?"

She didn't answer right away, but held his gaze with a question in hers. "Are you scared of me talking to him, Brock?"

"I'm not 'scared' of you talking to anyone. I just want to maintain consistency in the messaging."

She rolled her eyes at the phrase, which told him all he needed to know about what she thought of *messaging*. "We had a four-second encounter, and I asked him exactly one question, which is a question I usually ask almost anyone I'm interviewing, to start the process."

"Which is?"

"I asked about the single moment in his life that gave him the most joy."

For a moment, he tried—and failed—to imagine how his uncle, a man obsessed with his business and bursting with pride over everything he presided over, would answer that. His first million-dollar deal? Taking the business from his father? The day Blackthorne Gold won a World Whiskies Award? "What did he say?"

"He didn't," she said. "But he pointed to the keypad where I'd pressed eleven-o-eight."

"Their anniversary." It hit him hard, right in the gut. Why the hell didn't his uncle go to France and get that woman, then?

Because of that…secret?

Whatever it was, it had to be big.

"Were your brothers as grateful to be adopted by your aunt and uncle as you were?"

He drew back. "Rapid-fire conversation switch. Is that a trick your mother taught you?"

She gave a guilty smile. "She was a great interviewer, and, yes, keeping your subject off guard can be effective. And speaking of subjects, my dear subject, don't change this one. This isn't about me, this is about you."

He put his hand over hers. "Did you just call me your *subject*? Now there's a cold and unemotional way to describe your personal escort and Blackthorne door-opener. Not to mention your…"

"Don't." She flipped her hand and gripped his to stop

him from saying *lover*, because they both knew that he had been that for only one night. "Anyway, not that many doors have been opened yet."

After a beat, she laced her fingers through his, holding his gaze, making his mouth go bone-dry and his whole body unnaturally tight. Well, it was *natural*, he supposed. This close to a woman he knew tasted and felt like heaven? The rush of blood was more than natural.

"I'm still waiting for one more door to be opened." Her voice was low, sultry, and damn it, everything was getting tenser and...hard.

"Let me guess." He lifted their joined hands, bringing them closer to his mouth. "The door to ancient family secrets?" Or more recent ones?

"We'll get to that, but, no, not the door I want to go through right now."

Right then, the only door he wanted to take her through was the one to his bedroom. How the hell could he do that? He brought her hand to his lips, but didn't kiss it. "So what door do you want me to escort you through, Ms. Gillespie?"

He saw a little shiver roll her shoulders and shutter her eyes, confirming her body was reacting exactly like his was. "The Crazy Cow," she whispered. "Ice cream is my weakness."

He laughed and gave that kiss to her knuckles. "Vanilla or chocolate?"

"Salted caramel with fudge."

Yes, he needed cold ice cream, too. Because much longer and he'd need a cold shower instead. Pulling her up from her seat, he tipped his head toward the creamery. "Now that's one door I will open for you."

Chapter Ten

It was easy for Jenna to forget she was working while she was with Brock. The laughter and conversation were never forced, even when she threw him a tough question. The not-so-casual touches and one-heartbeat-too-long looks were thrilling enough that she would be lying to deny the attraction was as strong as the night they met and made love in the dizzying space of a few hours.

And that memory bubbled like a volcano deep inside her, threatening to erupt at any moment. Somehow, she'd have to hold off for three weeks.

But *how*? Three days would be a challenge with this man.

An hour later, they pulled into the small waterfront town of King Harbor, driving down a quaint main street with brick buildings and gingerbread Victorians on every corner. Jenna could only sigh with that delicious feeling of...letting go.

"It's something, isn't it?" Brock slowed at a light in town, stopping at a corner in front of a darling bed-and-breakfast, glancing toward the lacy wood railing and wooden rockers.

"Am I staying there?" she asked hopefully.

"You're staying at the Blackthorne Estate," he replied.

"Your house?"

He gave a quick laugh. "It's not exactly a 'house,' and there are more bedrooms than bars, which is saying a lot in my family. I meant this town is something."

"Oh, it is," she agreed, watching a few tourists cross in front of them and head into an art gallery. "I feel like I just stepped into…vacation."

"Right?" He gave her a satisfied look. "I knew you'd get it." Shifting into gear, he took the sports car at a respectably slow speed down the road, carefully avoiding groups of tourists and shoppers. "The minute I'm here, I feel different. All the edge of life fades away, and it's just…" He gestured toward the harbor, where boats bobbed on the moors with the sparkling Atlantic behind them. "Take a deep breath."

She did, getting a nose full of salt and sea and clean fresh air. "It's glorious."

"Put it in your book," he said, tossing her a smile. "It's the smell of…"

"Blackthorne?" she guessed on a laugh.

"Without the baggage," he replied, stopping at the next light and looking at her. "Without the branding and the business and the bottom line. This, to me, is the best part of being a Blackthorne."

"Elaborate, please. What does it mean to be a Blackthorne?"

He shot her a look. "We're not—"

"If you say you're not fascinating, I'll have to take a drink."

That made him laugh. "Well, you're in luck. We might be dull as dirt, but if you need a drink? Whisky flows like water at this place."

She gave him an appreciative smile as he shifted into

gear again and rumbled off the main road onto a side street, then another, then another. Before she knew it, they were on the edge of town at a massive gate, which opened as he pulled up to it, then started up a hill to reach the most stunning three-story, gray, gabled home she'd ever seen.

"Wow," she whispered, taking in what had to be a fifteen-thousand-square-foot home, with a zillion windows and a wraparound porch that offered unobstructed water views. Surrounded by lush acres of grass and gardens, the mansion was topped with a white widow's walk perched like a decoration on a breathtaking cake. "This is quite the summer home."

He downshifted the Porsche as they headed up the drive. "My great-grandfather bought the land and lived in the original house, which is now where my nana lives, right over there." He gestured toward a precious white Cape Cod-style cottage tucked into a garden. "My grandparents built the main section of the estate, which has obviously been added on to and renovated over the years, mostly by my aunt Claire."

"The main house is too big for your grandmother?" she guessed.

"Too empty, as she will no doubt tell you. This house used to be full from May to September, but now that everyone is an adult and running businesses, living in Boston and Kentucky and LA? It's hard to spend a lot of time here."

"Didn't you say you were just here for three weeks?"

"I was, but that was because…" His voice trailed off, and immediately she wondered if it had to do with Claire's leaving. "Phillip had a thing."

"A thing?"

He laughed. "A fund-raiser he was involved with,

and it just seemed prudent for me to work from here. Oh, my cousin Devlin lives in King Harbor, with his girlfriend, Hannah, in a cottage they just bought up in the hills. And Phillip lives at the estate when he's in town, but I'll bet my last dollar he's moved in with Ashley."

"His girlfriend?"

"Brand-new, but solid." He gave her a smile. "Phillip and Devlin both recently started committed relationships, so you get to meet their significant others, too, which is not a sentence I ever thought I'd say without irony."

"Why's that?"

"It's just that no one expected either of them to settle down, or my brother Jason or cousin Ross, but something must have happened this summer, because, wham, the four of them went down like dominoes."

Was it Claire's sudden departure? But Jenna had asked him enough about that subject for one day, so she limited her questions to the estate as he explained where the groundskeeper lived and told her about the couple who worked full time as the housekeeper and handyman.

"We have a chef on most nights in the summer, or we can go into town and eat."

"I'm not eating for a week after lobster and ice cream," she said as they pulled into a wide stone driveway that led to a separate garage large enough for more cars than she'd probably own in her life. "Oh, is that your grandmother?"

A white-haired woman wearing a blinding-green top and yellow pants was walking along the porch, carrying a watering can. She stopped to water a plant, then looked up, shielded her eyes from the late afternoon sun, and waved.

"That's my nana," he said, breaking into a smile. "You're going to love her."

She was going to *interview* her, but it seemed prudent not to mention that right now. "I can't wait to meet her."

He pulled the car next to a low stone wall and got out fast enough to round the front and get Jenna's door.

"Thank you," she said as she climbed out. "For me or the benefit of your grandmother?"

He made a face and pretended to dagger his heart. Then he smiled. "Yeah, both."

The older woman put down her watering can and walked toward the front, moving quite gracefully for an octogenarian. "Oh, Brock!" There was enough of a musical lilt in her voice that Jenna knew she was delighted to see her grandson. "This is an unexpected surprise."

"I should have called you, Nana," he said. "But we made an impulsive decision."

"*We* did?" Holding the railing, she came down to the drive, pinning a silvery-blue gaze on Jenna with no small amount of interest.

"Not only didn't I call, I brought a guest." Brock had to bend way over to kiss his teeny-tiny grandmother on a crinkly cheek, earning a warm hug around shoulders that dwarfed her. "This is Jenna Gillespie," he added.

"You don't need to call, honey. This is your home, too." She pulled back and turned to Jenna. "And your girlfriend is more than welcome."

"Oh, thank you, but..." Jenna glanced at Brock, expecting him to jump in and clarify who she was. But he let the misunderstanding go on for a beat or two, smiling a little and leaving Jenna to set the lady straight. "I'm not his girlfriend."

"Or whatever you kids call it these days."

Finally, he stepped forward and put his hand on Jenna's shoulder. "Jenna's writing a book about the Blackthornes."

Nana hooted a soft laugh. "I better have my own chapter."

"I hope you will," Jenna said, taking the old woman's hand in hers for a warm shake. "I'm here to talk to everyone and get a genuine understanding of what makes this family so special."

"Oh, we're neat, all right. Just like I like my whisky." She gave a gravelly laugh that revealed teeth far too white and straight to be anything but dentures. "If you want to know about this family, I'm the one to talk to. But I'm Fiona, dear. Not Mrs. Blackthorne. That's Claire," she added with an almost imperceptible sigh.

So, another person who missed the elusive Ms. Claire.

"I do want to talk to you, Fiona. I hope we can have many good long conversations."

She could have sworn she felt Brock stiffen next to her, as if he was ready right then to dive in and referee those talks. But Fiona looked utterly pleased at the idea, patting her silver hair that somehow seemed to make her eyes more gray than blue.

"Let's start right now." She took a step closer and slipped two hands around Jenna's arm, easing her closer. "I love two things in this life. Well, beyond my wonderful family, and right now you'll share both."

"They are?"

"Whisky and gardening," Brock answered for her. "But, Nana, I want to show Jenna the house and—"

"She'll see plenty of it." Nana flicked off his argument with a wave of a sun-spotted hand. "I'm taking this lovely lady to my garden for a stroll and a sip. Come

with me, dear. Brock will get your bags to your room."
She cleared her throat and muttered, "Or his."

"Oh, no, it's not…" Jenna looked at Brock for help
again, but he was frowning enough for her to know it
wasn't his grandmother's mistake about their
relationship that bothered him, but the fact that Jenna
would be alone without her Blackthorne chaperone.
Which was exactly what she wanted. "I'm sure we won't
be long," she said to him, then turned to the little
grandmother. "And I would love to see your garden."

Brock obviously knew better than to argue with both
of them.

As they made their way down a stone path to the
cottage they'd passed, Fiona tightened her grip, which
Jenna suspected was as much for support on the stones
as to express an unexpected amount of affection.

"What a delight to have family here," she said,
adding a squeeze. "Don't get me wrong, I love Joe and
Pam, they work here and keep such good company, and
it does seem like there's always someone coming and
going, but…" She added a sad smile. "Some days it
seems like more going than coming. Will you be here for
a while?" she asked with enough hope in her voice that
Jenna's heart cracked a little.

"I'm not sure," she said honestly. "I have a fairly
short window to do my research and write my proposal,
so I guess it depends on how many people I can talk to
here and how long it will take."

"Well, everyone in King Harbor will have something
to say about Blackthornes." They reached a white picket
fence that ran the perimeter of a garden exploding in
color. "Come with me," she said, opening the gate and
gesturing for Jenna to follow. "Let's get something to
drink and sit out in the garden." She slowed her step and

turned to look up at Jenna. "And by 'something,' I don't mean tea and honey."

Jenna laughed. "Sounds perfect."

Chuckling, Fiona led her up a few steps to a porch and through a screen door into the cool living room of a classic coastal cottage. White beadboard walls, weathered floors, and a comfy room full of embroidered pillows and golden afternoon sun created a warm and welcoming atmosphere.

"This is lovely," Jenna said, inhaling a mix of cinnamon and roses in the air. "Such a dreamy cottage."

"And so much more manageable than the big house," she said. "Don't get me wrong, I love that place, but it has Claire's fingerprints on every inch, and it's a touch more formal for entertaining and such. And it's so lonely most days."

"I can't imagine anything prettier than this." Jenna walked to a set of French doors that led to a back patio that overlooked the harbor and town below. "This is like a postcard."

"When Graham and I—the first Graham Blackthorne, that is—first got married, this cottage was all that was on the property. He wanted to build something much grander," she said, opening a glass cabinet filled with crystal decanters and glasses. "That Blackthorne pride wouldn't allow him to live in anything this small."

"Blackthorne pride?" Jenna watched her pour two generous glasses of the liquid gold she'd enjoyed with Brock. "I've picked up that it's pretty strong."

Fiona gave a sharp laugh. "Indeed. Pride is a character trait that runs strong in their DNA. It's their greatest charm and worst sin. It's what motivates them to compete to win, to be the best at whatever they do. It's also what blinds them to…" Her voice trailed off. "Outside, dear?"

"Sure." Jenna followed, tempted to whip out her notebook, but instinct told her there'd be time for something more formal. Now, when this talkative and lonely old lady had a drink and an audience, Jenna would get some of her best information. Her mother always said that a notebook was like duct tape on a subject's mouth.

They stepped to the side of the house through a white trellis into a garden that was clearly well loved. "You keep all this on your own?" Jenna asked.

"I get help with some of the heavier tasks when I'm planting from Joe, the handyman. But the daily upkeep does a body good. I can lose hours out here." She led Jenna to a grouping of chairs with a small table. "And I do like to have my four o'clock whisky right here and admire my work."

As she sat down, Jenna accepted the drink the woman handed her, glancing around to take it all in.

"Don't look too closely at those rhododendrons," she said. "They're giving me a time this year. But the larkspur's pretty, don't you think?"

"Everything is gorgeous. I can see why you'd spend hours out here."

"It's a lovely place to reminisce." Fiona held up her glass. "Here's to memories. I hope I can share some for your book."

"I hope so, too." Jenna beamed at her, taking a sip and still not used to the hot, smooth taste. "Brock told me this is the only whisky distilled up here in Maine."

She took a second sip. "And it was the first, made by my husband's father."

"Alistair Blackthorne," Jenna said, getting a little zing of excitement at the possibility of what Fiona might know about this particular piece of family history. "I've read a little about him."

"He was a great man, but he could be a son of a bitch if crossed." She grinned and took another drink. "Did you read that, too?"

"No," Jenna said. A son of a bitch who stole a recipe from the other distillery in town? "But I did read that he came over here with his wife, Meredith, from Scotland and brought the family trade of whisky making."

"Scotch whisky," she said. "Which is a whole 'nother thing from what you're drinking right there." Fiona leaned forward and sent a demanding glare over her glasses. "Except you're not drinking."

She smiled and lifted the glass. "It's potent."

"I should hope so," she said on a quick laugh. "Now where was I? Oh, yes, Alistair was a great distiller who lived to the ripe old age of ninety-five and is buried right on this property." Then she raised both white brows. "So be careful where you dig, dear."

Jenna swallowed at the warning. "For his grave?"

That earned a sharp bark of laughter and a pointed finger. "I like you. You're smart. So, here's my advice, pretty lass. Remember, there's a fine line between folklore and fact, especially when booze and Scotsmen are involved." She shifted in her seat. "It's not a line anyone would want you to cross."

As Fiona took a deep sip, Jenna inched closer to ask the next question. "Fiona, have you ever heard the rumor that Alistair Blackthorne stole the recipe that became Blackthorne Gold?"

She coughed a little, like the whisky had gone down the wrong pipe. "Yes, my dear, we've lived with that cloud over our head for years. Do us all a favor and dispel it."

Or prove it was true and have a nugget of gold that would sell lots of books and make Filmore & Fine very, very happy. Claire's leaving had potential, but what if this was the secret Brock's aunt announced she was tired of keeping when she walked out of her own birthday party?

"It's really the silliest old legend," Fiona continued.

"Sometimes they have truth to them," Jenna said.

"Sometimes," the old woman agreed. "But you'd have to find a Platt, and that would take an act of God."

Jenna immediately recognized the family name of Wilfred Platt, the owner of Salmon Falls Distillery and a contemporary of Brock's great-grandfather. "I assume they're all dead?"

"Good guess, although the conspiracy theorists say Wilfred disappeared one day and no one ever heard from him again. I think my son Mark once mentioned that he'd been in touch with a Platt, though I can't be sure."

"Can't be sure of what?" Brock walked into the garden, holding Fiona's whisky decanter in one hand and an empty glass in the other. He filled the glass, refilled Fiona's, then took a seat next to Jenna, stretching out long legs clad in khaki shorts that revealed muscular, dark-hair-dusted calves.

"Can't be sure of ancient history," Fiona said with a smile. "And I'm giving her a lesson in the one thing she needs to know about this family."

"Don't tell me," he joked. "Blackthornes are proud."

"Pride is a good thing," Fiona said, swirling her whisky. "Until it's wounded."

Frustrated that Brock had shown up and somehow managed to change the subject, Jenna turned back to

Fiona. "You were saying your son Mark was in touch with the Platt family?"

After just one sip, Brock put his glass down and stood. "We better get going, Jenna. It's about time for Nana's afternoon nap."

Whoa. Was that because his father was mentioned, or because he didn't want her near this Platt family history? He couldn't keep her from it forever. But she stood, not wanting to argue the point now.

"Can I come back and visit you in the next day or two?" Jenna asked, hoping to do that without an escort.

"My dear, I'm here every day and every night. All alone." She added a meaningful look to Brock. "I hadn't expected it to be quite this quiet this summer, but with Claire gone…"

"We'll be around," Brock said quickly, putting a hand on Jenna's back to lead her out. "You get some rest now, Nana. Bye."

Jenna blew her an impulsive kiss, which made the older woman laugh, then let Brock usher her to the front.

"I'd love to show you around the house now," he said.

"Maybe later? After I get in my room, I have a little research to do."

He slowed his step. "Jenna, I guarantee you that you're wasting your time pursuing this stolen-recipe angle. It's a dead end."

She searched his face and could have sworn she saw that same glimmer of fear. "I'll be the judge of that."

His jaw clenched just enough for her to know that if she depended on him, she'd get nowhere. She had to think of some way around that.

But if she succeeded in uncovering the truth and the recipe was stolen, she could kiss Brock Blackthorne goodbye...which was probably a better option than kissing Brock Blackthorne for fun.

But for the moment, there would be no kissing, just lots and lots of hunting for the truth.

Chapter Eleven

"**S**o the ugly rumor is true. You *are* in town."

Brock gave his barstool a little spin to come face-to-face with his oldest brother, Phillip, who sauntered across one of the many boldly patterned rugs that added to the luxurious atmosphere of the Vault. But his words didn't subdue the sound of happiness in his brother's voice, which matched the gleam in his eye when he glanced at the woman on his arm.

"Brock!" Ashley broke away from Phillip to reach out and give him a warm hug. "How awesome that you're back so soon."

He gave Ashley a quick embrace and held up knuckles to Phillip. "See? That's the way you greet someone, dude. Not 'the ugly rumor is true.'"

Phillip laughed. "She'll teach me manners eventually. But, seriously, you just left King Harbor after almost a month. Is there another brand crisis I don't know about up here?"

"Oh, there's a crisis, all right," Ashley teased, giving him a playful jab with her elbow. "Nana told me all about her."

Brock drew back. "What did she tell you?"

"That you brought a beautiful woman and looked a little, I don't know, what was the word she used, Phillip?"

He glanced away from his conversation with the bartender. "Smitten. The word was smitten."

"Nana's drunk," Brock joked. And weirdly perceptive.

"As if that's even remotely possible." Ashley slid onto the barstool next to him, flipping back some dark hair and giving him a smile Brock had known since he was a freshman at Harvard and Ashley was the resident advisor in his dorm. To think that girl was now a permanent fixture at his brother's side might have surprised him fourteen years ago, but now Brock saw they belonged together.

"Anyway, we'll decide for ourselves when she gets here," Ashley finished.

Brock shook his head, certain he hadn't heard her right. Jenna had told him she was staying in for the night, taking the chef's offer of a light dinner delivered to her room. She promised him they'd get an early start in the morning, when he would bring her over here to tour the Blackthorne Distillery, adjacent to the Vault.

So Brock had come to the Blackthorne-owned pub alone, certain he'd run into people he knew, hoping that would get his mind off this woman who'd blown into his life and turned his schedule—and thoughts—upside down.

"She's not coming here," he said.

Ashley gave him a look that was downright pitying. "Honey, I just saw her climb into the back seat of Devlin's Audi, and their parting shot was, 'We'll see you at the Vault.' We stopped by the estate to check on Nana, and Devlin and Hannah had done the same thing. We met her and invited her along."

"She doesn't know I'm here."

Ashley jabbed his shoulder. "Shouldn't have let her off-leash, big guy."

No, he shouldn't have, but he couldn't exactly keep her prisoner. Well, then, let her be surprised when she walked in, determined to do her backdoor digging for dirt, only to find the very man who had control over her shovel.

Except, right that minute, he felt...empty-handed.

Phillip joined them, handing a glass of wine to Ashley and adding a kiss on her hair. That got him a return smile that could light the room.

"So what's the deal with this woman?" Phillip asked, leaning on the bar to keep an arm around Ashley. "Is she going to rip the Blackthornes to shreds in this book or what?"

"Not if I have anything to do with it." Except, she seemed to keep finding workarounds to the brick walls he tried to put between her and anything he didn't want her to know. Problem was, without knowing Aunt Claire's "secret," he didn't even *know* what he didn't want her to know.

"Oooh. Pained expression." Ashley reached up and patted his cheek. "Haven't seen that look since Kayla King blew you off for the Harvard second-string quarterback."

"And now she's a reporter on ESPN. It was a good move for her." He glanced to the door, already anticipating Jenna's expression when she walked in and saw him there. Would she be exasperated? Surprised? Happy?

"Look at him," Phillip whispered the comment into Ashley's ear. "Totally watching the door."

Brock glared at his brother, waiting for the age-old

resentment and distrust to rise up. But Phillip had changed so much in the last few weeks that Brock couldn't conjure up anything like that.

Fact was, Phillip didn't even seem like the same guy who'd been so messed up right here in this bar not so long ago that Brock literally had had to drag him out on his drunken ass. But it wasn't Brock who'd finally talked sense into his oldest brother, it was the woman next to him.

"Can you blame him?" Ashley asked. "She's awesome, Brock. We talked to her for a while."

Great.

But he leaned a little closer to Phillip to change the subject. "Hey, question for you. Do you remember Dad talking to someone who might be connected to the old Salmon Falls Distillery?"

"No, but…" Phillip frowned and inched back. "Please tell me that crap isn't coming up again. When the hell will someone put that stupid stolen-recipe trash where it belongs?"

Until someone definitely disproved it? Never. "But why would Dad talk to one of them?"

"Old case, maybe?" Phillip guessed.

That would make sense, since his attorney father had been the head of Blackthorne's legal department. "Does the name Platt ring a bell?"

Phillip shook his head. "Ask someone in Legal. And if it wasn't a Blackthorne Enterprises deal, maybe it's in his private papers. Pretty sure that when we remodeled the fifty-third floor in Boston, they sent boxes of crap to the estate, and they're probably up in the attic. You should shut the haters up, man."

Brock couldn't agree more. The old gossip would rise up periodically, and he'd find ways to shut it down, but the stain was on the brand like spilled whisky on the barrel-and-thistle logo.

"Of course, every year at this time someone brings it up," Phillip added.

Brock nodded, knowing that the anniversary of King Harbor's Founder's Day was always ripe for rumors like that. Someone dug up old tales, and the "Blackthorne Gold was stolen" nonsense always emerged.

Phillip pointed over Brock's shoulder, a slight warning in his eyes. "Incoming, bro."

He couldn't help it, he turned to look just in time to see Jenna share a laugh with Hannah, who strode in, hand in hand, with Brock's cousin Devlin.

They all sure looked…comfortable. So maybe Jenna hadn't been yanking open closet doors, looking for hidden skeletons. Or maybe she had, and no one even realized it, because she was that good.

And beautiful.

He felt his eyes shutter closed as he shook his head, resigned to the constant hum of need the minute he saw her. Just then, she spotted him, her lips forming a cute little O in surprise. Or was she? He'd mentioned going to the Vault that night when they were driving into town.

Either way, it didn't diminish the light in her eyes as she came forward. He slid off his barstool to greet her with a hug that felt as natural as it did good.

"So much for holing up in your room to work," he teased.

"First of all, it's not a room, it's a suite fit for a queen. Second…" She gestured to the others. "How could I resist this invitation?"

Brock reluctantly let her go to greet his cousin Devlin and give a brotherly cheek kiss to Hannah Reid, whom he'd known for years, since her father had been a master craftsman at Blackthorne Boatworks before being unceremoniously let go by Graham a while back. But Devlin had rehired him, and it seemed any bad feelings about the firing had been wiped away by this very serious romance that had come up as fast as a rogue wave for these two seasoned sailors.

They fit next to each other like there'd never been any space or rivalry between them, and Devlin looked even more chill and comfortable in his own skin than ever.

"They saved me," Jenna told Brock on a laugh. "I'd run into your grandmother again after I brought my dinner tray down, and she suggested an after-dinner drink and, wow." Jenna laughed. "Does that lady have a hollow leg or what?"

"Two." Brock laughed and offered her his empty barstool. "How about another?"

"Just water, please." She settled in and looked up at him, capturing her lower lip between her teeth. "Not mad I slipped out, are you?"

He just held her gaze and gave his head a slow shake. "Mad is not the word I'd use."

"Surprised?"

"Starting to realize that nothing you do surprises me."

"Then you're happy to see me."

Who could lie in the face of those deep-blue eyes and that irresistible smile? He was ridiculously happy. Like, way too happy to make sense. "The better to keep an eye on my crafty little researcher."

That made her let out a delicate laugh that somehow drew him closer. "Your family has given me no secrets, you'll be happy to know, but…"

But? He felt his eyes widen as he looked at her, bracing for God knows what his grandmother might have said.

She whispered into his ear, "I found a Platt."

He felt the hairs on the back of his neck rise and not just because her warm breath tickled. "Excuse me?"

"A guy named Roger Platt, who lives in Buxton, which is not far from Salmon Falls, which is…where I'm going tomorrow."

"Excuse me?"

"Nana said there's a Range Rover in the garage with keys in the ignition for guests to use, or Joe the handyman could drive me, or I could Uber if I—"

He held up his hand to stop her. "I'll take you, Jenna. You don't know Maine roads. Joe would talk your ear off—"

"I want to hear what Joe has to say."

"But I want to take you." Even as he said the words, he knew how much he meant them.

"I don't need a babysitter," she said, reaching for the water the bartender had placed in front of her.

"I'm not a babysitter."

"Or an escort. Or a roadblock. Or a distraction."

He let out a sigh, not wanting to be any of those things. "How about a…partner?"

Her look was pure skepticism.

"I'm serious," he said. "I'd very much like to meet this Platt guy."

"So you can make sure he doesn't tell me anything that would make for a page-turner?"

He shrugged. "The truth is, I believe right down to my last strand of DNA that this rumor is fake, that this is revisionist history driven by jealous competitors and people who can't stand how successful the Blackthorne family is. Let's find out the truth and put that hundred-year-old gossip to bed once and for all."

She held his gaze for a long time. Long enough for

the music and noise to fade. Long enough for Brock to get a little lost in eyes the color of the Atlantic when a storm was brewing. Long enough to know that the only thing he really wanted to put to bed was Jenna Gillespie.

"And if it turns out you're wrong?" she asked.

"I'm never wrong."

"Careful, you might choke on that Blackthorne pride, Brock David."

He gave a slow smile, coming closer. "You know what it does to me when you call me David?"

She reached up and touched her finger to the side of his glasses, pushing them up a tiny bit. "Answer my question. If this rumor is based on fact and that whisky you're drinking was born from a stolen recipe, what will you do?"

"I don't have to answer that, because I know it's not."

She angled her head, a warning look in her eyes. "I did find some pretty interesting things."

"A reference to it in an article in *Forbes*? That reporter had a beef with my uncle."

She wrinkled her nose, making him guess she'd thought that was an ace in the hole. "There are other things."

"The documentary on the history of Maine that has exactly thirty-three seconds on the subject, found at the fifty-four-and-a-half-minute mark?"

"Well, yeah."

"Producer is currently in jail for sexual assault and has zero credibility."

"But there was also—"

"A blog entry from ten years ago on King Harbor Founder's Day about the 'secrets of the harbor'?" he guessed, knowing exactly what it said.

She stared at him.

"Did you get to the part that says there's a Loch Ness-style monster out there?" He pointed toward the harbor. "Sensationalism put out by a misguided tourism director."

Her narrow shoulders sank. "Okay, but I still want to meet this Roger Platt."

"So do I," he said. "And then I'll prove to you I'm right."

"On one condition," she said, leaning forward.

"Of course I'll wear my glasses and you can call me David."

She laughed. "I meant you can't try and stop me if we find out there's truth to the rumor. I'm going to track it down. You can't put up...*Brock* walls and road*brocks*."

He laughed. "The woman has a way with words."

"I mean it, you can't."

"If I do..." He slid his arm around her waist. "You'll have to take those walls down."

"Brock by Brock," she teased, inching closer and getting right in line for a kiss he could give her in two seconds flat.

"Darts, you two." Devlin clapped a hand on Brock's back. "Loser buys, so I hope you brought your hard-earned cash, little cousin."

Brock glanced at Jenna, lifting his eyebrows. "You want to know about the Blackthornes? The good, bad, and the ugly?"

Devlin leaned in to add, "I'm good, Phillip's bad, and once you see Brock throw a dart, you'll have no doubt who's ugly."

She laughed. "I'd love to watch."

"Watch?" Brock put his arm around her again, loving the feel of her against him as he slid her off the barstool.

"You're my partner, and, God, I hope you have better aim than I do."

With the music of her easy laugh in his ear, they joined the others in the private game room, where, of course, Brock lost miserably. But he hadn't had so much fun in years.

Chapter Twelve

The minute they were off the main highway out of King Harbor, heading northeast into the heart of Maine, Jenna understood why Brock had chosen the Ranger Rover instead of his Porsche for the forty-five-minute excursion to find Roger Platt.

The big vehicle bounced along rutted state roads surrounded by thick woods broken by dirt paths through acres of farmland.

"Do you need me to plug an address into the GPS?" she asked.

Brock turned to shoot her a disbelieving look. He'd taken off his sunglasses not long after they'd started driving as thick clouds formed, and with his contacts in, she could see right into his deep, bottomless brown eyes. And hated to look away.

"To Salmon Falls?" he asked. "I could get there and back in my sleep. I have a few times, to be honest."

"First of all, we're going to Buxton. Second, in your sleep?"

"Salmon Falls is part of the Saco River and essentially a village on the outskirts of Buxton. And for teenagers anywhere in the fifty-mile vicinity? It's a mecca in summer. The falls, the cliffs, tons of swimming pools. Did you bring a suit?"

"Uh, no."

"Then you'll have to swim naked." At her reaction to that, he laughed. "Just kidding. Kind of."

She couldn't help chuckling. "You're awfully happy and relaxed for a man about to find out that the cloud over his family might…break into a storm."

He put his hand on her arm, his fingers warm from the wheel. "It is going to storm, based on this sky, but if I'm going to stick with your weather metaphor, I'm so happy that we are finally going to dispel that cloud once and for all. I should have done this years ago. As far as I'm concerned, this is very important brand-management work, and I'm grateful to you."

She smiled, knowing some of the things she'd read sounded awfully credible.

"Plus, I'm in Maine. Life is easier here."

"Then why don't you move here permanently?"

He shrugged. "It's a bitch in the winter, for one thing. For another, there's Blackthorne Enterprises to think about."

"And you do think about it."

"Not going to lie, Jenna, I love the company as much as the family. In my mind, they're one entity, and I told you how I feel about being a Blackthorne. It's a responsibility, yes, but one I relish. Don't you relish your job?"

"I…do." She knew she sounded less than enthusiastic. "I love writing stories about people, weaving in history and emotions, but…it's not all I want out of life."

"What do you want?"

At the intimate tone and the way he touched her

hand, she could hear a far too honest answer bubbling up. *A guy like you.*

"I want a family," she admitted without any shame. "I want what I saw you have with your brother and cousin in the bar last night. To be surrounded by..." *Love.* She didn't have the nerve to say that, though. "To not be lonely."

"Well, whatever the opposite of lonely is, that's how I grew up," he said.

The opposite of lonely. She tucked the phrase away, planning to use it somewhere in her book. "What's that like?"

"It's like wondering if you'd ever get an hour that wasn't interrupted by a sibling or cousin who wanted to do something."

"I guess the grass is always greener," she mused, but felt his gaze on her again, so she finally met it. "No one ever wanted to do anything with me. My big thrill was letting my mom rehearse interview questions on me, which is how I learned this job."

He gave her hand a sympathetic squeeze. "What's she like?" he asked, turning on yet another almost dirt road, away from a massive cornfield.

"Haven't you ever seen her on TV?"

"Yeah, when I was younger. And..." He made a face. "I might have watched a few YouTube videos the night we went to dinner."

"Of my mother? Why?"

"To know you better," he said without a second's hesitation. "Hey, you're not the only one who's curious." He threaded their fingers together, a move that was way too personal and romantic, but Jenna had zero desire to pull away. "I want to know what makes you tick."

"I'm boring," she said with a sly smile.

"Take a drink." They said it in unison, the thrill of that little inside joke and the warmth of his hand making her giggle.

"Seriously. You grew up in New York, right? Only child? Tell me about little Jenna May Gillespie."

She let her head drop back on the headrest, sighing. "I can't imagine how to explain being an only child to someone who grew up with a house full of brothers and cousins. Two houses," she corrected. "And so folded into a family basket that even the tragedy of losing your parents made you love that family more. Did you realize that was happening when you were little?"

He eyed her. "Is this how you talk about yourself?"

She gave a guilty laugh. "I don't like to talk about myself. I was raised to consider it bad manners."

"Were you raised to consider not answering questions bad manners? I asked. I'm interested. Fascinated, even."

The timbre of his voice reached way down to something inside of her, warming her, encouraging her to tell him what that life was like. But he'd never understand, and it would sound like she wanted pity.

"Jenna?" he prodded, stroking her knuckles with this thumb. "One thing. One deep, insightful real thing. It's only fair, considering you're taking my life and family apart to turn it into mass entertainment. This is just us. You and…David."

She knew that. It was why she held his hand and enjoyed the contact right down to her toes.

"Okay, *David*. But I did just tell you something. Being an only child is lonely."

"I can imagine."

"No, no." She practically cut him off, leaning forward to make her point. "Being an only child of

119

career-driven parents who worked sixty, seventy, eighty hours a week and entertained VIPs the remaining time was…" What was a word that was worse than *lonely*? That captured the total solitude of her childhood? "It was…empty."

"Oh."

"See? Pity party. I knew you'd throw me one. This is why I didn't want to share my life and upbringing."

"Okay. No pity, I swear. You were on your own a lot. I bet that's made you independent and strong and resourceful and fearless."

"Is that what you think I am?"

"Yeah," he said with a nod, as if he'd just realized all that. "Also gorgeous, funny, smart, and, holy hell, do you look good soaking wet. Also naked."

She laughed, leaning her head toward his shoulder because he made her a little dizzy, or maybe that was the butterflies doing acrobatics in her stomach. "You're…funny."

"I'm serious. Love that naked, wet look on you." He smiled. "So let's recreate our rain date with a trip to the waterfall when we're done here."

Oh God. Everything in her wanted to say yes. *Everything.* "Are we almost there yet?"

"You sound like Logan on a road trip." He lifted their joined hands and pointed to a green sign that said Buxton was in two miles. "Now plug in Roger's address, and let's do whatever it is you do."

"I'm doing it alone."

"What?"

"Brock, you can't walk up to the guy and tell him who you are. He'll never be honest with me."

He snorted, and she imagined all the arguments he was readying up. "I'll tell him I'm David…Smith."

120

"I'm not going to lie to a source," she said. "I'll tell him I'm writing a book on the Blackthornes and researching history." She tapped her phone and entered the address into the GPS. Then glanced around, frowning. "Oh wow. We're already here."

"What do you mean?"

"This is his property. But I don't see a—*ahh*! Watch out!" She shrieked as a man stepped right out into the road, forcing Brock to slam on the brakes, kick up dust, and stop about four inches from the end of a rifle barrel. "Oh my God."

"Welcome to the backwoods of Maine," he muttered under his breath, opening the window to stick his head out. "Excuse me, sir, but—"

"Get off my property!" The man was huge, at least six three, with a red beard and wearing camo from head to toe.

"Sorry," Brock called, holding up his hands as if he needed to show he was unarmed. "We're looking for Roger Platt."

"He ain't looking for you."

Brock let out an exasperated sigh. "Leave?" he asked Jenna.

She almost choked. "Are you kidding? We just got here."

"Jenna, this isn't New York. It's Maine. It's backwoods. It's—"

She opened her door very slowly, also holding up her hands as she stepped partway out. "Are you Roger Platt?" she asked.

"Jenna." Brock tried to grab her hand, but she slid just out of his reach, standing partially protected by the SUV's door.

Steely gray eyes narrowed. "Who's askin'?"

121

"I'm Jenna Gillespie. I'm an author and biographer, and I'm writing a book about the Blackthorne family."

He flinched at that, but never shifted his gaze or opened his mouth.

"I believe there's a...connection between the Platts and the Blackthornes."

"Who's that with you?"

"That's...David." Not a lie, not technically. "My driver." Also true.

The man's sizable chest rose and fell a few times with slow, considered breaths. "What do you want to know?"

"I just want to talk about..." She swallowed, took a breath, and lifted her chin. "The recipe."

She could have sworn she felt Brock bristle from where he sat.

"'Bout damn time someone showed up." He lowered the rifle and jerked his head for her to follow. "And for the love of God, you better write somethin' that opens up their checkbooks. We ain't had a Blackthorne payment in thirteen years, and we're runnin' dry out here."

Brock's jaw nearly hit his chest. And not just because the man, whoever he was, had just lied through his yellow teeth. Jenna was going with him?

He shot out of the Range Rover, slamming the door and taking a few strides to head her off before she went into the woods with a guy carrying a shotgun.

"What are you doing?" He put a hand on her shoulder, firm enough to slow her step.

"You can come."

"Oh gee, thanks."

She gave him a look, then leaned closer to whisper, "I know you don't like what he just said, but—"

The man, now twenty feet ahead, turned around. "Hurry up."

Brock gave him a vile look. "I have a bad feeling about this, Jenna."

"He's not going to hurt us," she replied.

"And you know that how?"

"He wants money," she said simply, quickening her step to keep up with the man as the wooded path ended, revealing a vast cornfield with stalks so high they towered over Brock's six-two frame.

He took an inhale and recognized the smell immediately. "Sugar gold corn," he said. "This is what Blackthorne Gold is made from."

The man stopped at the edge of the cornfield, turning to eye Brock. "It's what Sweet Willie is made from."

"Sweet Willie?" Brock frowned. "I've never heard of that. Is it a whisky?"

"'Course you never heard of it. Blackthornes made sure of that."

Brock almost tripped at the shot of resentment that went through him, but Jenna grabbed his hand as if she anticipated his reaction.

"What's Sweet Willie?" she asked.

"Best damn liquor you'll ever taste in your life. Of course, if you drink Blackthorne Gold, you'll recognize it."

Jenna squeezed Brock's hand in warning, enough to silence him while they wended through what felt like a thousand rows of cornstalks, which broke for an occasional dirt road, then picked up again. It took ten, maybe fifteen minutes of nonstop walking.

"Over here," the man finally said, pointing to the last clearing.

As they stepped out of the wall of cornstalks, Jenna sucked in a soft breath. "Oh, that's pretty."

On a hill overlooking the fields stood a classic and massive log cabin with dozens of windows and about six cars and trucks and a bunch of motorcycles—two Harleys and a Ducati, to be precise—parked in front.

It definitely wasn't where Brock thought this mountain man would live. And whoever owned that fleet of expensive vehicles had some serious cash.

"House used to be a lot nicer," the man said. "Then the payments stopped."

What payments? Brock bit back the question and followed the man away from the house, down another path, stopping when they reached a barn. The words *Sweet Willie* were burned into the side of the weathered wood, and the entire left side of the grass in front of it was filled with wooden crosses in what looked like a graveyard.

He hoped like hell that wasn't where they ended up today.

"It's in here," he said, walking to a large door secured with a combination lock. "Can't use the old distillery, of course. It's haunted. But this works for our needs."

Haunted? Brock damn near choked before he opened his mouth to say something, but once again, he deferred to Jenna's pleading look.

"Wait right there," the man said, leaning over to work the combination lock. He slid the door open just enough to stuff his large frame through, then closed it again, leaving them standing outside.

"Jenna." He spoke through gritted teeth. "I don't

know what you think this is going to accomplish, but that guy's a lunatic with a gun."

"Do you or do you not want the truth?"

"You think you're going to get that from *him*?"

"As soon as you heard 'Blackthorne payment,' you decided he wasn't credible."

"Maybe, but what shred there might have been disappeared with the 'haunted' distillery. Oh, and…" He gestured toward the cemetery.

"They all say Platt," she said, ignoring his call for rationality. "We're at the right place."

"If we were in a bad B movie."

"Brock, please."

"What? I'm here, unarmed and ready for whatever. What's your goal in this?"

"To find out if the recipe is stolen," she said.

"You're seriously going to believe this guy?"

She didn't answer, because the door slid open a foot, and Rifle Man came back out. The gun had been replaced with a flip-top glass bottle filled with liquid that was a very familiar amber.

"Taste it," he said, holding two paper cups in one hand, then pouring with the grace and flair of a seasoned barkeep.

Brock put his hand on Jenna's arm before she could reach for a cup, though he didn't think she was actually going to do that. "Hang on. Who are you?" he said to the man.

"Roger Platt. And who are you?" the man demanded. "And don't give me no lie, 'cause I can tell you're one of them. They all have the same arrogant, smug expression."

"I'm Brock Blackthorne," he said.

"You his missus?" the man asked Jenna.

"I'm exactly who I said I was," she replied. "A writer looking for the truth. I'm writing a book about the Blackthorne family for Filmore & Fine. Have you heard of that publisher?"

He shrugged, unimpressed by the famous book publisher's name.

"Was the recipe for Blackthorne Gold stolen?" Jenna asked.

He snorted. "Ain't got no proof of that—"

"As I suspected," Brock said, putting his hand on Jenna's back. "Let's get out of—"

"But we did get checks for one million dollars a year signed by a Blackthorne."

Brock froze mid-step, staring at the man. "Excuse me?"

"According to my granddad, the money started showin' up every January, startin' right after my great-granddaddy Wilfred *mysteriously* disappeared back in the '30's."

The emphasis left no doubt who he thought was responsible for that disappearance, which sent a punch of anger through Brock.

"Well, *my* great-grandfather didn't steal the recipe," Brock said. "I've seen the paper that he wrote it on. I know his handwriting."

Roger lifted one meaty shoulder, forcing Brock to tamp down more fury.

"There are pictures of him distilling the whisky at our King Harbor operation," Brock ground out. "Journals that cataloged how they tested each step of the process, how they tried different flavors for the burn, soaked the barrels in exactly the right formula, and used techniques perfected by my ancestors in Scotland. We have documented proof that Blackthorne Gold is our family recipe."

The other man shook his head, letting Brock's speech hang in the humid air for a moment, then he closed his eyes. "Come in here."

Brock glanced at Jenna, who gave a nod, and they followed him into the dimly lit barn, where familiar scents bombarded Brock. Vanilla, oak, and sweet corn mixed with the smell of aged, burned wood. The smell of the distillery he'd practically grown up in.

In the corner, a small still was humming with life, mashing the corn and puffing out steam.

Five or six barrels lined one wall, each with a tap.

The man shoved an empty paper cup into Brock's hand. "Take a pour. Any one of them. Tell me you ain't tastin' your Blackthorne Gold." He practically spat the words.

Brock rumpled the cup. "No, thank you."

"What about the payments you mentioned?" Jenna asked. "What were they for?"

He turned to flip the valve on one of the barrels and filled yet another cup. "Only person who knows that is old Willie himself, and they ain't never found his body. My guess is that it's somewhere where Blackthornes bury people they want to shut up. Then they pay hush money to keep the family from—"

"That's garbage." Brock squeezed the tiny cup in his fist, feeling that vein in his temple pulse.

Jenna stepped closer. "If the money stopped coming, why wouldn't you do anything about that?"

"Like call a lawyer?" He snorted. "Blackthornes would bury us in legal costs."

"Or call a newspaper," she suggested. "Why not set the record straight about the stolen recipe? Your missing ancestor? Why hide this all these years?"

He gave her a long look. "Kinda hoped the money

would start up again." He grinned at Brock. "Is that why you're here, Blackthorne?"

Fat chance.

When Brock didn't answer, the other man stuck the glass under Brock's nose. "Smell familiar?"

As familiar as his name.

"Let's go, Jenna." He eased her back with a little force. "Now."

On a sigh, she came with him, as if she knew arguing was fruitless. Brock led her out the door into the heavy, storm-laden air. Even this air smelled like his childhood, his life, his family, his name.

Could Alistair have stolen the recipe and paid the family off for decades and no one knew that? And what happened to Wilfred? Was that hush money or had Blackthornes been blackmailed for years? And how the holy hell did he not know any of this?

Outside, the clouds had gathered and thickened, and the air was rich with rain about to fall. And they had to find their way through that damn cornfield, because Brock couldn't take one more minute with this lying son of a bitch.

Silent, still holding the detestable bottle, Jenna took his hand and went with him into the cornfield. Ten feet into the first row, he had to face two facts: The recipe *might* have been stolen, and he had no freaking idea which way to go.

Chapter Thirteen

"**B**rock, we're lost." Jenna had waited a good fifteen minutes before stating the obvious and really wouldn't have said a word, because she trusted Brock to get them out of this field, but then she heard thunder, and that was a game changer.

"Not...exactly." He stopped when they reached one of the paths that didn't seem wide enough for a car, but had to be a way out. Except the last three they'd followed had taken them...nowhere.

He wiped some sweat from his brow and adjusted his glasses. "I can't believe I got out of the Range Rover without my phone."

"I left mine, too." At the next rumble, she made a face and looked up at the cloud-covered sky. "That storm isn't far away."

He exhaled and put his hands on her shoulders. "Guess you're furious I made you leave that outstanding interview."

"I was for a minute."

He lifted a brow.

"Okay, five minutes. I did want to pepper that guy with questions and..." She lifted the bottle. "Compare."

"There's no comparison," he said. "But I didn't trust myself to stand there and listen to that crap any longer."

"There's more to the story, Brock. And I thought you wanted to put an end to these rumors."

"I do. And now I'll go back to King Harbor or Boston and start looking into who paid his family for so many years and claimed it was Blackthorne money. We have a top-notch security team who can look into it. And he's right about the lawyers. He won't know what hit him."

And then you'll cover it all up, Jenna thought. "Maybe it *was* Blackthorne money."

"Do you seriously think I wouldn't know about that? Or have heard something? I'm at every board meeting, Jenna. Nothing goes on at that company that one of my brothers or cousins or uncle doesn't know about, and no one would keep something like that a secret."

"Even Claire?"

He drew back. "Do you think… No. It's impossible. It's—"

A clap of thunder made her jump. "Getting closer." She glanced around, her heart sinking. "Brock, this is pretty much the most dangerous place in the world in a storm. Please. I don't want to die for this book. Can we find shelter?"

"Okay. This way. I think we're getting closer to Salmon Falls."

"Why there?" she asked as the first fat drops hit their heads.

"There's shelter," he promised, taking her hand. "Might be a challenge to get inside, but if it hasn't changed too much in fifteen years, I think I can do it. Come on."

She clung to his hand as he picked up speed and weaved them through the rows of corn, the sweet smell mixing with the fragrance of the drizzle as it picked up intensity, the sound of thunder getting closer every moment.

But then they stopped, and it wasn't thunder she heard, but one solid noise of rushing water, even louder than the rain.

"We're close," he said, taking off his glasses and clipping one arm in the collar of his T-shirt. "I know where I am now. I can find the distillery from here."

"Another distillery?"

"The original one," he said.

"The *haunted* one?"

"Ghosts or lightning, babe. Take your choice."

She curled her lip. "I'll take ghosts."

They headed toward the sound of the water, but before they reached the falls, he detoured into some woods. The rain picked up to full force, soaking her hair and shirt, sluicing down her face.

He stopped for a second to look around and listen, then helped her through an overgrown trail, up a hill, and finally they reached a structure that made the earlier barn look like the Taj Mahal.

Two stories, with a smokestack that went up about twenty feet, the building looked like it had been beaten with an anvil. The first floor was gray and black brick, covered in mold and filth, and the second-floor windows were nothing but gaping holes. Vines covered most of one side, and a tree had fallen into the building at some point and crushed part of the roof.

"Welcome to Salmon Falls Distillery," Brock said dryly.

"We are *not* going in that building."

"Okay, then we're staying out here." Mother Nature punctuated that statement with a crack of lightning that split the blue-gray sky with one long, bright white bolt that literally sent chills up Jenna's arms.

With a soft scream, she grabbed on to him. "No," she muttered, smashing her face against his chest just like she had the other night. Only this wasn't nearly as...thrilling. "I'm scared."

"Of the storm or the shelter?"

"Both."

"I won't let anything happen to you." He wrapped his arms around her and pulled her against him, both of them soaking wet. "I know how to get in the basement, which is as deep as the structure is high. We'll wait out the storm there."

The *basement*? Could this get any worse?

The next crack of lightning answered the question, and she followed him toward an ivy-covered wall. There, he shoved away some branches and leaves, revealing a sliding wooden door that he took her through.

She blinked at the darkness, broken only by a little bit of light coming from the second floor through rotten floorboards and a rusted staircase that was missing most of the treads. The walls were gray and moldy and featured a good amount of graffiti and were no doubt home to all kinds of critters.

"Come on," he said, wrapping a protective arm around her. "Watch your step, but I know where I'm going."

"You've been in here before?"

"The teenage trips to the falls might have included some grown-up version of hide-and-seek."

"I'd rather die." With the next bolt of lightning and damn near simultaneous thunder, she thought she might.

"I hid with a, uh, friend."

She slowed her step and pushed back a strand of wet hair. "You brought girls here?"

"The more adventurous ones," he said on a soft laugh. "But not nearly as frequently as Phillip, trust me."

They made their way over deep cracks in the foundation, most of which were home to thriving weeds. At the stairwell, he stopped and looked down a good twenty or more steps.

"You think I'm going down there?"

"I think…" Lightning flashed, and a punch of thunder shook the whole building, perilously close. "It would be safer there than here." He took her hand and started down. "It's just a barrel room. Come on."

Grasping his hand, she followed, squinting into the darkness as they descended into a room lined with whisky barrels and covered with dirt. When they reached the bottom, she realized just how buried they were, looking up at a filthy wooden loft that had to be twenty or more feet above them.

"That's where they aged the whisky," Brock told her, following her gaze, then he brushed off a barrel that had been cut in half and sat down, pulling her onto his lap. "There's no safer place in a storm, I promise."

But, oh Lord above, she felt anything but safe. The storm, the building, the man. Nothing felt safe.

He took the whisky bottle from her hand and set it on the ground as another deafening clap of thunder echoed above them. Automatically, she wrapped her arms around his neck and buried her face against his shoulder. Any other girl would be thrilled to be smack up against this man with his wet T-shirt clinging to biceps and abs. Any other girl would be laughing at the adventure, straddling him with abandon. Any other girl would…not be Jenna Gillespie.

With each roll of thunder, she gripped tighter, too terrified to be ashamed of how she trembled and the tears she fought.

"Jenna," he whispered, stroking her hair. "It's just a storm."

There was no such thing as *just a storm*. It was a dark, horrible, agonizing memory that flashed into her brain with the same clarity as each bolt of lightning.

"Aren't you afraid of anything?" she asked.

"Heights," he answered without hesitation. "Anything over ten feet makes me dizzy and sick and pretty much want to die."

"Then you get it."

He eased her back a little, searching her face, only inches away. "Bad experience?" he guessed.

She swallowed and nodded. "Really bad."

"Want to tell me?"

Oh yes. She did. But up to that moment in her life, she'd never told anyone. Not even her parents. They'd just be riddled with guilt, and nothing could be done now to change what had happened. Plus, it sounded distant and ancient and as silly as the possibility that this building was haunted.

He put a warm, tender hand on her cheek, stroking lightly. "You can trust me," he said. "Maybe it would help to talk about it."

Maybe. Or maybe she could just cuddle closer into his sexy body and let that big strong hand find more of her to touch.

She breathed in at the reaction that thought sent through her body, and the move just pressed her more into his lap and chest.

"Tell me," he urged, putting his lips over her hair as

he whispered the words. "What happened? It always helps to talk about it."

"When I was about six years old," she said softly, a little stunned that the words were coming out at all. "A nanny locked me in a closet during a storm."

"Ooof." He grunted in disgust. "I hope she was fired and had her license revoked."

"I never told my parents, but she left soon after, so it didn't happen again."

"Why didn't you tell them?"

She thought about the question, one she'd pondered many times in the middle of the night, especially during stormy nights. "I didn't think they cared."

He just stared at her. "Your mother and father?"

"They both loved their jobs more than…"

"Than they loved you?"

She shrugged. "It felt that way to me as a little girl. In retrospect, it was stupid. But it left a scar, and I've been terrified of storms ever since."

"You know what you need?" he asked, stroking his thumb over her jaw.

Yeah, that. She needed that. "Therapy?"

"A new memory involving a storm."

"We could get drunk on Willie's whisky."

"Or we could get drunk on…" He slid his thumb under her lip and started working his magic there, drawing her lip open and touching the inside, stroking with a finger that she already knew could make her scream. "Each other."

"We already made a memory in a storm." As protests went, it was weak. And so was she.

"Let's make another one." He closed the space between them, lightly brushing her lips with his, then adding pressure to intensify the kiss. Instantly, heat coiled through her, traveling up her back just like that lightning, crackling over her skin, setting off sparks in her head and thunder rolling way, way lower.

Oh yeah. This was already a good memory.

With a groan of pleasure, he shifted her on his lap, sliding his hand down her throat and over her breastbone.

"Your heart's racing," he murmured, dragging his mouth over her jaw and throat.

"And my head's light."

"See? Drunk," he teased, sliding his thumb down the V-neck of her collar, then plucking the wet cotton off her skin. "And soaked."

"Mmm." She pulled back enough to see him, to thread her fingers into his wet hair and ruffle it. "David in the Rain."

He lifted his brows in question.

"That's what I was calling you in my head that night. In the cab and the bar. David in the Rain."

"We're good in rain, you and me."

She smiled and kissed him again. "You could make me forget all the bad stuff."

"Oh yes, I could." He slipped his hand under her T-shirt, his palm searing her back as he rubbed up and down.

Underneath her, she could feel him grow harder, making her want to rock her hips and give in to the need deep inside her. Silently giving him permission, she arched her back, inviting his touch, offering access to her throat and breasts.

He took it. He thumbed her nipple to a painful, tender, aching point that felt attached to every nerve ending in her body. She kissed him again, letting their tongues dance and curl around each other, the only sounds their tight, short breaths and the blood pumping in her head.

"You don't need that fake whisky," he murmured into the kiss. "Just this, Jenna." His hips rose and fell, inviting her to slide her leg over him and wrap her thighs around him.

His hands were everywhere, hot and sweet and talented, on her ass, up her back, into her hair. She bowed her back and closed her eyes, hearing a whimper from her throat collide with a deep groan from his.

As he eased her top higher, she opened her eyes, looking straight up, lost and dizzy and disoriented as he slid his hands under her bra and made her bite her lip. Her gaze landed on the loft high above them, the three or four feet of rotten wood planks holding what looked like half a dozen whisky barrels.

"Your top is soaked." He reached behind her to unclasp her bra as she caught sight of something... familiar. Something out of place. Something upside down. She blinked as her night vision kicked in and let her read the words.

Was that the barrel-and-thistle logo that was on all things Blackthorne?

She frowned, squinting into the darkness, barely able to make out the words that seemed to be branded into the wood, also upside down. Did that say...

"Wait. Stop."

His fingers froze as they spread over her breast. "Okay," he said in a raspy voice. "Second thoughts?"

She straightened and turned around to read the words from the right direction. "Do you see that barrel?"

He choked a soft laugh. "Not exactly looking at the scenery, Jenna."

"Well...I think you might want to." She pointed to

the words and logo. "Up there. The barrel in the back."

He inched to the side so his gaze could follow her finger. "I see about seven of them, and I promise you there's no whisky in them. If you're dying to drink from that bot—"

"Read it. The one in the middle." She looked at him, narrowing her eyes, while that little buzz of excitement she got when something that felt like a good story thread tugged at her gut.

Silent for a moment, she watched as he scanned the area in the filthy loft, as interested in his reaction to what she'd just read as what it meant.

"I don't see..." He blinked. His jaw clenched. And he mouthed the words she'd struggled to read upside down. "Platt Blackthorne Distilleries. Contents: Platt Gold Whiskey." His face screwed up as if something was wrong in the universe, and it wasn't that *whisky* was spelled with an e. "*What?*"

He eased her off him without taking his eyes off the offending words. She went easily, getting to her feet and snagging the wet T-shirt he'd just taken off her.

Silent, moving as if he were wading through molasses, he took a few steps, staring up at the loft. There were wooden two-by-fours nailed to the wall as steps, but the first six or seven looked like they'd been ripped away.

"Holy hell," he whispered, going closer, his head all the way back as he looked up. "There is no way—"

"That's your logo."

"—that I'm going up there."

"I will," she said, coming closer. "I'm not afraid of heights."

"I can't even watch you go up there," he said, walking to the wall to eye the two-by-four rungs that led up there, the first one much too high to reach from the ground.

"But…Platt Gold?"

He flinched as though the violation of the brand name actually hurt him. "I guess if I…" He grabbed an empty barrel and rolled it closer. "If I stood on this, I could reach that rung and climb." He snorted. "Or I could put a gun to my head and be happier."

"I swear I can do it," she said.

She saw that vein in his temple pulse and his Adam's apple move as what she suspected was a surge of Blackthorne pride ran through him. "I'll try."

He hoisted himself onto the empty barrel and reached the bottom "rung." There, he pulled so hard, Jenna could see his muscles bunch as he swung up and got his footing.

"Be careful," she muttered, pressing her knuckles to her lips as he managed to get up a few more rungs, and his head cleared the loft.

His response was a slow, ragged breath as he kept his gaze locked on the offending barrel. "Son of a…it really *is* our logo." He grabbed the edge of the loft and hoisted himself again, but as he did, a loud crack echoed, and the board he held splintered off, hanging by a nail.

"Brock!" she screamed as he dropped, dangling with a tenuous grip. Swearing hard, he grabbed another piece of wood and saved himself from falling.

"It's not worth it," she said, knowing how much that had to have shocked the system of a man who hated heights.

For a long moment, he said nothing, but after a sigh, he started to lower himself back down. "Yeah. You're right."

When he got to the ground, he stood still, his face bloodless, but his eyes sparking with fury and fire.

"The storm's over," she said softly.

"Good. Let's get the hell out of here."

"You think this place is haunted?" she said, desperate to lighten the moment.

"I think…" He stabbed his fingers into his hair and dragged his hand through it as he stared up at the loft. "Some things are better left alone."

Which would be the opposite of what Jenna thought, but she didn't want to stay in this place or put him through one more moment of personal misery. So she followed him back to the stairs, and with the storm subsided, they found their way to the road where he'd left the Range Rover.

It wasn't until they were almost back in King Harbor that Jenna remembered the bottle of whisky she'd left on the floor.

Chapter Fourteen

"Nothing? Not a single appearance in any file anywhere of the name Platt?" Frustration and something that felt a lot like a kick in his ass tightened Brock's voice on this, the tenth call he'd made on the drive home from Salmon Falls. And who could blame him? Every single attempt to get to the bottom of this had come up with nothing.

Next to him, Jenna had been listening to the conversations on the speakerphone, quietly tapping her cell phone, no doubt doing her own online search. Then John Rand, the top attorney at Blackthorne Enterprises, had called back.

"We can do a digital search all the way back to 1989, Brock. That word or name doesn't appear anywhere," John told him.

"What about the non-digital files? The older files that haven't been digitized?" He flipped that piece of the puzzle around and around, but it didn't fit anything. None of this did.

The possibility that his great-grandfather really had stolen the recipe for Blackthorne Gold? Or...*Platt Gold*. With the logo Brock revered stamped right on the barrel?

"Anything over thirty years is in storage," John said.

"Of course, we could arrange to go through it, but fair warning, it could take months."

"*Months?*" He shot a look to Jenna, who made a face that reflected his frustration. For different reasons, of course. He was sure she didn't care about the history or the brand or the whisky in a barrel, but she could have a decent story on her hands.

"There were a lot of files sent directly to King Harbor," he added. "Before my time at Blackthorne Enterprises, but I do know that there were several containers of private documents and files that were your, uh, father's. If memory serves me, they were transported to the family estate in Maine not long after he passed."

"That's what Phillip said. Okay. And, John, if you find anything, anything at all with the name Wilfred or Roger Platt, any Platt, let me know ASAP."

"Sure thing, Brock. You want me to alert Trey or Graham?"

Not until he got to the bottom of this. "I'll handle that."

"They'll both be up there soon for the Founder's Day stuff," John added. "So if I find anything, I can save the messenger costs and have them bring it."

Founder's Day. When the Blackthorne Gold float went up and down the middle of King Harbor with…pride. And the Platt name had been…buried in the basement of an abandoned distillery?

"Sounds good, John." After he signed off, he heard Jenna sigh.

"Find anything?" he asked her.

"Not a word about Platt Blackthorne Gold. Do you think you could find those files of your father's?"

"That's where we're going next."

Not half an hour later, Brock led Jenna to the back

staircase behind the kitchen, grateful that no one had been around when they got back to the estate. At the top of the third flight was a plain wooden door that most people wouldn't even notice, but Brock knew exactly where it led.

Taking Jenna's hand, he opened it to a plain set of wooden stairs. "These are a little steep," he warned, hitting the switch for the overhead light. "And the third one has a creak that will make you think you're going to fall through, but you won't."

She laughed. "You do know your way around."

"I played hide-and-seek in this house on every rainy summer day from the time I could count to ten. Logan always went up here because there's a door in the attic that leads to the widow's walk, and he knew I'd never go out there to get him."

"So you've always been afraid of heights," she mused.

"That's *not* why I quit today. The floorboards…" At her look, he had to laugh. "Okay, it's *partially* why I quit."

"Trust me, I get fears. Any deep-seated reason like I have?"

"No," he admitted as they reached the top of the steps. "Just your garden-variety irrational fear." He ducked into the massive storage area, hot from the summer sun already beating through the roof and rafters.

The place was about forty feet long and twenty feet wide, spanning most of this wing of the house. Pinpoints of light streamed in through thin vents and one long, skinny window, the sunbeams highlighting a bit of dust dancing as they moved through and disturbed the peace.

For an attic, it was fairly organized, considering his aunt Claire had long ago transported the family memorabilia to Maine, claiming the attic in the Weston house was too small. The estate housekeeper kept this one clean, and her husband, Joe, had built shelves to hold stacked plastic storage bins. The middle of the room was filled with a smattering of holiday decorations, retired lamps, and some furniture. And seven well-defined bins and paraphernalia that didn't need a label for Brock to know which one belonged to which Blackthorne.

The model boats and yacht-racing trophies were Devlin's. The ridiculous collection of Hot Wheels and other toy race cars had Ross's fingerprints all over it. The row of binders was Trey's coin collection, and about a hundred VHS tapes of old movies had once been Jason's pride and joy.

He turned to Jenna, about to tell her where he guessed his father's files would be, but stopped at the sight of her eyes bright, her head swiveling, a smile threatening to stretch across her face as she reached to a clothing rack sagging under the weight of dozens of Halloween costumes.

"Remind me later that you're happier in attics than basements," he teased.

"I wasn't…unhappy in that basement." She lifted a Power Rangers cape and fluttered the corner of a SpongeBob SquarePants shirt he'd rocked one chilly October. "It's just that this is…" She swept one hand to the left and one to the right. "Like a gold mine for me."

He got that. "Blackthorne family history central," he agreed. "And you're welcome to peruse our diplomas and christening gowns and that whole bank of yacht-racing trophies. But now we're looking for legal files."

It didn't take long to locate the blue-topped containers labeled simply MB. Jenna settled on an old chair while Brock pulled the bins down, one at a time, scanning the shelf. "I'm counting seven. No, eight. Is it too hot up here for you? I can carry them down."

"Let's just start looking. Anything that says the name Platt."

"Yep." He plopped on the wooden floor next to her and opened the first lid, which revealed nothing but long brown case files full of legal-sized documents. He let out a grunt. "This could be tedious."

"Or the most fun I've had in…" She lifted a file and winked at him. "Hours."

"We'll get back to that," he murmured, putting his hand on hers. "Assuming you don't find out some dirty truth and tear off to write it and publish it."

"Brock." She angled her head, a little sadness in her eyes. "I know what this means to you."

"And I know what it could mean to a book about my family."

She didn't answer, slowly opening a file.

"You did come digging for dirt," he said.

"I told you what I want. Color. Depth. Truth. None of that has to reflect poorly on this family."

"What if it does?" he asked, still holding her gaze.

"We'll cross that bridge," she said, fluttering the first page. "This is a patent filing."

"So's this," he said, taking the next file. "Maybe we can skip this box."

"Maybe we should check to see if Platt filed a patent."

He let out a breath. "Of course. You're brilliant."

"Trained by the best."

The best? He snorted as he took the next file, unable to hide what he thought of parents who let her be taken care of by an abusive nanny.

"They aren't monsters," she whispered, as if she'd read the thought behind his derisive noise.

"Your nanny was. And you were..." He closed that file and took the next. "Lonely."

"Says the man who longed for solitude."

He glanced around the attic, practically smelling moments from his childhood. "But I had constant support. Someone—usually three or four or five someones—always had my back. In a game, at school, at home, through...the worst times." He ran a finger over the words *Mark David Blackthorne, Attorney at Law* at the top of a page.

"You have the same middle name as your father," she said, staring at his hand.

He looked up. "You know, he was a lot more like David than Brock."

"Tell me what you remember most about him."

He thought about that for a while, finishing with the last file in this bin, another patent registration, then closing the lid to move on to the next one.

"He loved my mom a lot." The admission surprised him, but it was what came out first. "I never really thought about them as...a couple. They were just Mom and Dad, a unit. But..." They laughed a lot. Had inside jokes. Probably found ways to escape and be alone and... "I'm glad they died together."

She sucked in a breath, her eyes wide. "You are?"

"Not glad they died, or that I lost both parents in one accident. But I like thinking that they're..." He shook his head, suddenly realizing how he sounded. "Anyway, he was a good guy, and they had a great marriage, I think." One exactly like he'd want if he...

At the thought, he froze with his hand on a file. Why was he thinking about that? "What about your dad? What's he like?" he asked quickly.

"Distant. Distracted." She lifted the top page of a file.

"Why is this blank? And this? And this? Why file a bunch of blank pages?"

"Try another one." He looked at the next file. "These are my dad's personal taxes from thirty years ago. You were saying?"

"I was saying…" She smacked her hand on the armrest of her chair and slid onto the floor next to him to show him the file. "Holy crap, Brock. Look at this."

He squinted at the paper, one page with photocopied images of checks all written to "PFT." Each one in the amount of one million dollars. He just stared at the four on one page, unable to speak.

Very slowly, she lifted the page to show four more check images. And the next page, and the next.

"Look at the dates," she said. "One every January, all from a personal MD Blackthorne account."

At the bottom of the stack of what had to be well over twenty million dollars' worth of checks, all signed by his father—until the dates hit the 1960s, and those checks were signed by Graham Blackthorne, Brock's grandfather.

The pages of check images ended, then he spied a handwritten ledger that looked like it predated those. Down one column, the letters PFT. Then the amount of one million and a check number, going back decades, all the way to… He flipped the last page and finally reached the end.

"The first check was written on January 1, 1934." Brock shook his head, doing the incredible math.

"The month after Prohibition ended," Jenna said quietly, reaching into the bin to pull out a very thin leather folder that was tucked into the side of the bin. Holding it gingerly, she set it on her lap and placed a tender hand on it, as if respecting its age and history. "Can I open it?"

"Of course," he said, scooting to get even closer. "Let's see what it is."

She slid the book onto his lap and slowly lifted the aged cover.

The first page was yellowed stationery, the edges curled by time, with the embossed heading *The Honorable Justice Martin J. Harkham, York County Court* at the top.

His gaze skimmed the letter, landing on one line...

The legal formation of The Platt Family Trust (PFT) for the purpose of financial transaction...

"We found the Platts," she whispered.

The Platts, who'd been paid more than seventy million dollars by his family.

"What do you think?" she asked. "Hush money or blackmail?"

He let out a sigh. "Either way, I think I'm staring at a big, ugly, permanent stain on my family name."

To his credit, Brock had no interest in hiding the truth or burying the past. He seemed to want to get to the bottom of the Platt situation as much as Jenna did, but only because, as he'd said repeatedly, he didn't believe the recipe had been stolen.

Well, if someone had paid more than seventy million for it, then, no. Not *stolen*. But that meant *Blackthorne Gold* wasn't *Blackthorne* at all. And that was just as bad to Brock.

After searching the rest of the boxes and finding nothing else related to the Platt family, they packed up the folder and ledger and headed to the one person nearby who could shed some light on what they'd discovered.

Fiona was in her garden, humming while she pruned, delighted to see them.

"Can I get you a drink, dear?" She slid an arm around Jenna's as if they were fast friends.

"I don't think—"

"We need help, Nana," Brock said, no time for niceties. "And it's serious."

She turned her lips down and leaned into Jenna. "He was more fun when he was little," she said on a loud whisper.

"Nana." Brock was having none of her chatter. As soon as he settled her in her favorite chair, he told her everything that had happened, from the sugar gold cornfields, to the discovery of the barrel—thankfully leaving out how Jenna had spotted it—and the million-dollar checks that had been drafted and mysteriously stopped thirteen years ago.

She listened without a question, her aging eyes remarkably clear as she processed the news and studied the evidence. Finally, she leaned back and let out a shuddering sigh.

"I always suspected there was…something."

Neither of them spoke, waiting for more.

"A few times, during an occasional lean year, I heard my husband fighting with a lawyer he only spoke to by phone. He wouldn't ever take or make those calls at the company, but in his private office at home. I never knew what or who he was talking about, but there was one line item that got paid, no matter how thin profits might be."

"Do you know the name of the lawyer?" Jenna asked.

"Most likely Bill Whitlock."

"Is he…available?" Jenna braced for the news that this lead was long dead.

"Oh my, yes. He was a very young man back then, and now he lives right here in King Harbor."

Brock leaned forward, frowning. "Why have I never heard of this guy? A lawyer who did work for Blackthorne Enterprises?"

"Because he didn't do work for Blackthorne Enterprises," she said. "He did work for your grandfather, privately. Then, once your father became an attorney, he took over."

"We should talk to him," Jenna said to Brock.

He nodded, but his gaze was intent on his grandmother. "Anyone else? Any other ideas, Nana?"

She took a long, deep breath and shifted all her attention to Jenna. "I've been thinking about you," she said, surprising them with the switch of topics.

"That's...nice," Jenna said with an uncertain smile.

"I am wondering if you're worthy..." She glanced at Brock, and instantly a slow heat crawled up Jenna's chest, no doubt deepening the color in her cheeks. Was she worthy of Brock? Is that what—

"Not of my grandson!" Fiona said with a soft cackle of laughter. "He'd be damn lucky to have you."

Jenna didn't quite know what to say, but felt better when she saw Brock's amused smile, the first since they'd left the attic.

"I'm wondering if you're worthy of knowing...the past." Fiona gripped the armrests of her chair and pushed herself to her feet. "I think you are."

Jenna looked up at her, confused.

"Come," Fiona said, flicking her fingers, then turned that hand to point to her grandson. "Just Jenna. Alone."

He didn't argue as Fiona guided Jenna back into the house. As they walked through the living area to the back bedrooms, the older woman put a hand on Jenna's back and led her to a small guest room full of classic antique furniture and dizzying flowered wallpaper.

"This is where I keep Meredith's journals."

Jenna's jaw unhinged. "Meredith Blackthorne? Alistair's wife? She had journals?"

"Three of them." She ambled to a closet and opened the door, pointing to a top shelf. "The leather books, up there."

When she nodded her permission, Jenna reached up to get them, her heart racing a little at what incredible insights she might find on the pages.

"Does anyone know you have these?" she asked as she drew three thick, ancient journals from the shelf, holding them as if they were literal gold, not just *literary* gold.

"Graham—my husband, not my son—gave them to me before he died," she said. "I've read some, but mostly I..." She perched her narrow frame on the edge of the bed. "It's not all pretty, our old history. It's not all bad, either."

Jenna gripped the journals, rubbing her palm over the top one, knowing that whatever was in here, it would likely make the basis for at least the first third of a book, giving her an unprecedented insider's view into this family's deep roots. This little pile of the past could essentially guarantee a book proposal that would be accepted and a book that would be published. In here, she could find the good, the bad, and the...buried.

"Do they say anything about the Platt family?" she asked.

"I haven't read them all. The first one covers Alistair's decision to leave Scotland and start a new life in America, and I've skimmed it. It's romantic, to be honest. He left to keep Meredith happy. The third one is the last part of her life and includes her thoughts about her son and me, which is all that I ever was interested in." She added a soft chuckle. "She hated me at first. By the time she made her last entry, she'd have picked me over him."

Jenna smiled back, having no doubt this spry, colorful woman had won over many hearts in her lifetime.

"The second one is the thick of the business, after the bootlegging days, into the 1930s and '40s. That wasn't so interesting to me."

Jenna nodded, her heart rate ratcheting up at how interesting it would be to *her*. "Do I have your permission to reprint and quote from these?"

Fiona stood slowly and took a step closer, placing her cool, parchment-smooth hands on either side of Jenna's face. "You may read them, and use them, on one condition."

With the next breath trapped in her chest, Jenna waited, a little afraid of Fiona's price. "Which is?"

"Don't hurt him."

"You mean…Brock?"

"Well, I sure as hell am not worried about you hurting Alistair," she joked.

But Jenna didn't laugh. "Why would you think I'd hurt him?"

"Because you can't love Brock Blackthorne casually or temporarily."

Love? "Fiona, we've only just met."

"Please, dear. I'm damn near ninety years old. I know what I see between you two."

"That's just…" *Lust.* "A warm friendship."

Fiona rolled her eyes with the finesse of a teenager. "Call it what you want, dear, but I've never seen Brock look at anyone quite the way he looks at you."

The words had an unexpected effect, nearly weakening Jenna's knees. "He's probably…worried I'll tarnish the brand."

"If he's worried, it's because that man knows what it feels like to lose someone you love and doesn't want to go through it again."

Jenna blinked in surprise at this new psychological profile of Brock. "Because of his parents?" she guessed.

"Oh yes. He's buried that pain for years, covering it with all his flag-waving over all things Blackthorne. And, yes, his aunt and uncle took care of him—as did I, I might add—but I think, deep inside, he believes that love means loss."

"I'll keep that in mind," Jenna said softly, pulling the journals to her chest.

Fiona put her hand on the journals and eased them away from her. "You'll do more than that," she said. "You will give me a promise, swearing on whatever it is that matters to you, that you will not let my grandson fall in love with you only to lose you."

Jenna just stared at her.

In the moment of silence, those gnarled fingers closed around the leather-bound books, and Fiona managed to slide them free of Jenna's hands. "If you can't make that promise, you can't have these journals."

Could she promise that? Or that if he did, she'd never leave him?

Fiona fluttered a few pages, enough that Jenna could see the handwriting inside. Meredith's handwriting. As good as having the long-dead woman in front of her for an interview. Everything in her itched to get her hands on them again. But…

"Fiona," she whispered. "I just met him a few days ago. I can't, in good conscience, tell you I can stop him if…if…" She swallowed, knowing better than to use a euphemism with this woman. "If he falls in love with me."

"Then don't let him fall in love with you." She held the books out to Jenna, tempting her and adding a lifted brow. "But if he does, you can't hurt him."

"What if I can't keep that promise?" she asked.

"Then your book will never see the light of day."

Jenna knew better than anyone how easily—and how late in the game—that could happen.

"So, yes or no for Meredith's journals, dear?" she asked sweetly, as if she hadn't just negotiated Jenna right down to the mat.

She wet her lips, closed her eyes, and reached for the books. "I promise," she whispered.

Chapter Fifteen

Brock whipped the dart through the air with what felt like master precision, watching it twirl, spin, and hit the edge of the board and fall to the floor of the private game room in the Vault.

"Dude." Phillip snorted from a few feet away, scooping up his darts to take his turn. "You're worse than usual, if that's possible. Too much Jenna?"

Not *enough* Jenna. "Long day, is all." Was it just this morning they were stuck in a storm, making out like teenagers and finding buried secrets?

"Where is she?" Phillip asked.

"Working," Brock said, remembering the light in her eyes as she clung to those journals and begged off to her room after dinner.

"Watch this." Phillip took his spot in front of the dart board and set up his stance. He threw a look at Brock just as he let go of the dart, which, of course, hit the dead center of the board. Phillip cracked up. "Like taking candy from a baby."

Brock rolled his eyes and didn't even bother to watch the next dart, looking down at his half-empty glass of Blackthorne Gold, his brain straddling two problems: missing Jenna and wondering about…Wilfred Platt.

He eyed his brother, who pumped his fist after his third straight bull's-eye. "You *sure* you don't remember Dad ever talking about someone named Platt?" he asked. "Wilfred or Roger? Maybe a trust by that name?"

"You asked me that already." Phillip ambled to the board to retrieve his darts, then approached the table, eyeing Brock. "Is that what's bugging you? The Salmon Falls crap? I know you'd freaking slit your own wrists before you let something bad be written about Blackthornes."

Brock didn't bother to disagree.

"Unless you are thinking with the wrong brain, my friend." He slid onto the barstool at the high-top table, one of a few in the private room. "It happens, of course, to the best of us."

"I don't believe Alistair stole the recipe for this…" He lifted the glass. "Any more than I think there's a man in the moon. But something weird happened with that family. I trust Jenna to find the truth, and I'll help her."

"Then why aren't you helping her now?"

Good question. She'd been distant ever since leaving Nana's. He chalked it up to her fascination with the journals and determination to start reading them. But maybe it was more than that. Maybe she was planning to do some damage to the Blackthorne name. Or…his heart, which had no business getting involved in these thoughts, but there it was.

For a long time, he stared at his drink, then at Phillip. "How'd you know?" he asked softly, not that the few others in the room could hear them.

"What was bothering you?"

"That Ashley was…you know."

Phillip made a face that told Brock he knew exactly what that meant. "She just fit, I guess. In the sack, in life, when things are smooth and when they suck. Ashley just fits right…" He hit his chest with his fist with a noisy thud. "Here."

All Brock could do was shake his head. "Didn't take long."

"Fourteen stupid years," he reminded Brock. "But those years got us to where we belonged." He lifted his glass in a toast. "Have I thanked you enough for putting that woman in my life back in college, however begrudgingly you did so? She's so flipping awesome, I…" He laughed. "I'll give you the game. You can't afford to lose any more tonight."

Brock snorted and clinked his glass, throwing back the rest of the whisky, not caring right that moment if the recipe was stolen, bought, or made by elves. It tasted great.

"Speaking of my woman, I'm headed back to her now." Phillip stood and pushed his chair in. "You need a ride?"

"I'm going to walk," he said. "Thanks."

A few minutes later, Brock made his way through the back streets of King Harbor, off the beaten tourist path, taking a shortcut he'd used a million times to get to the estate. A full moon slid out from behind some clouds, spreading light to make it easy to find his way. He checked the time as he neared the gate.

Not quite midnight. Would she still be up? Want company? He looked up at the house to see if the lights were on in her room, but his gaze was snagged by the widow's walk perched at the top. There, silhouetted in the moonlight, was a woman.

A casual observer might imagine that was a ghost from long ago, a seafarer's wife looking out to the Atlantic, waiting, wondering if she'd be a widow. But he wasn't casual, not when it came to Jenna Gillespie.

He stood stone-still and stared at her, watching her look up at the moon as she lifted her hair and let it flutter over her shoulders. He imagined the sound of her sigh, the silkiness of that hair, the way she'd feel in the cool night air bathed in moonlight.

Of course she'd be somewhere that he couldn't—or wouldn't—go. Still, drawn like a magnet to her steel, he headed into the back of the house, rounded the corner into the kitchen, and climbed the attic stairs. When he reached the one that squeaked, he stepped hard, hoping she'd hear him coming and meet him halfway. At least in the attic. Not...up there.

But she didn't open the door, probably not as in tune to his arrival the way Logan had been when they played hide-and-seek. In the attic, he needed his phone flashlight to find his way to the tiny door that led to the widow's walk, noticing around him that more boxes had been opened.

He glanced at a set of sports trophies and yearbooks and a photo album that had BB on the cover. So she'd found his bin and looked through it.

Far from feeling any kind of violation, he felt the thought send a weird shot of adrenaline through him. She cared about the family, and she cared about him.

Slowly, silently, he opened the door and peered up the last seven steps to the walk.

"Hey, Rapunzel. Come on down."

"Brock? How did you find me?"

"I spotted you from half a mile away." He stepped closer, cringing at the stairs he knew would take him to a place that made him dizzy.

And a woman who made him dizzier.

"Come on up," she called, then appeared at the top of

the stairs, wearing nothing but a thin tank top and cotton sleep pants. "I'm lonely."

Oh man. "Come to me. I hate it up there."

She just smiled. "You made me run through a storm in an open cornfield today." She reached a hand toward him. "Face your irrational fear, Brock David. The view is gorgeous from up here."

His gaze dropped over her again, his breath hitching at the sight of her hardened nipples through the top and the silhouette of her thighs in sheer pants. "It's gorgeous from down here, too. Come to the attic, and let's…play."

"Hide-and-seek?" she asked on a laugh.

"I was thinking more along the lines of spin the bottle."

She let out a sigh that he couldn't interpret, but it sounded mighty wistful. "Probably not a good idea."

Neither was going up there, but if it was the only way to get next to her? He put his foot on the first step and swallowed. "I might have to close my eyes when I get up there, but…" *I'll use my hands.*

With careful steps, he made his way up, slipping her into his arms when he ducked through the narrow opening to the widow's walk.

"Good job," she whispered, looking up at him. "Now check out the view."

He searched her face, her big blue eyes, and bowed lips. "I am. It's beautiful." Pulling her into him, he let their bodies press, top to bottom. "Missed you tonight, babe."

She stayed silent, but her eyes said it all. She missed him, too.

"I lost at darts," he admitted.

"Don't blame me for your lousy aim."

"I drank some whisky, made from a possibly stolen recipe."

"Nothing I've read yet tonight confirms that. The only weird thing I found was that Meredith seemed a little afraid of seeing someone called The Duke."

He frowned. "My barber in Boston? Dude's old, but that would make him well over a hundred." He stroked her face, lost in her eyes for a moment. "What else did you find?"

"A beautiful love story. A commitment to family like I've never seen. And enough drama to make a decent movie. Or...book."

"Good for you. The whole night, I've been thinking about...this." He lowered his head and kissed her mouth, lightly, barely a touch, but it sparked and made him want more.

She stood still for a second, hesitating, holding back, then very slowly lifted her hands to close them over his arms. She squeezed and then dragged her hands over his shoulders, giving an appreciative moan and angling her head to get more of the kiss.

Instantly, they molded together, her curves against his hardness, her hips pressed to his, their hearts hammering a matching beat, chest to chest.

"I gotta say," he murmured into the kiss, "these heights are dizzying."

"You never come up here?"

"I'd scream for Logan from the bottom of the steps. But I always found him."

He added a squeeze, pulling her into him, letting her feel what she did to him.

She dropped her head back with a noisy sigh, just like the one he'd imagined. "You found me," she whispered. "Now what happens?"

"Whatever..." He tipped her chin so his lips could find their way to her throat. "You..." He slid his hands up and down her back and sides, painfully aware that the tank top was the only thing she wore, and it was as thin as air. "Want."

She bowed her back, and once again, he grew hard, his body seeking hers, his hands already sliding under that top to touch her warm, smooth skin.

"Brock, we…can't."

"Brock who?" he teased, rounding her rib cage to run his thumb over the sweet, soft underside of her breast. "Don't make me go to my room and get my glasses." He inched his head back, but let his hand cup her, watching her eyes close and her jaw go slack with pleasure. "On second thought, let's go straight there." He kissed her and rocked against her. "Now."

"Oh." The word was pure agony and didn't reflect at all the ecstasy he was feeling. "Brock."

"David," he insisted.

She eased back, blinking, focusing, finding his gaze. "I can't do this."

He stilled his hand, slowly moving it away from the precious breast he wanted to caress all night. "Can't or won't?"

"Honestly, can't." She flattened her hands on his chest with another sigh, this one more frustration than sensual. "I want to," she added. "I want to so…damn… much."

"Oh man, I hear a 'but' right around the next corner."

She nodded. "But I made a…" She swallowed. "Ethical commitment to my publisher. It would go against…everything."

"You should go against everything," he said, pulling her back into him. "Starting with me. Ending with me, too."

She blew out a breath, and he could see the torment

on her face and feel the chills on her skin. "You have no idea how much I want to."

"Then what's stopping you?"

"Not what. Who."

He drew back. "I swear to God, your publisher will never know. Our secret. Our..." He rubbed his thumbs against her ribs. "Our little secret. And, babe, you already know how good it's going to be. Better now that we actually know each other."

She bit her lip, and he watched the agony in her eyes, the longing and lust and internal battle to do what both of them wanted.

"There's more on the line now than there was the night I met you, Brock."

He looked at her, considering exactly what that was. Genuine feelings. Truly caring about each other. Trust. Risk. "Yeah," he agreed. "Which is why I want you even more."

She blinked at the admission and swallowed. "Brock, we—"

"We fit each other," he finished, echoing his brother's confession, a little shocked at how right that was.

Her eyes flashed. "We do?"

"Physically," he said quickly. He didn't want to scare the crap out of her by letting her know just how much she was starting to mean to him.

"So, why can't we wait?"

He could think of a million reasons why. "Wait for what?"

"The book to be done."

His jaw fell. "You think I'm made of titanium? I couldn't spend that much time with you and..." He frowned, trying like hell to interpret the look in her eyes and failing. "What brought this on, Jenna?"

"I told you the day I found out who you are that we couldn't do…anything. I told you."

"But this afternoon, in the distillery, I was pretty sure you'd changed your mind."

"It was…the storm."

He lifted a brow. "So the only time we can make love is during a storm?" He looked up at the sky. "Lightning, damn it!"

But she didn't laugh. "Let's just wait."

He inched back. "Until the proposal is accepted?"

Laughing softly, she nodded. "Yeah. That'll work."

"Fine. But I get to show you what you're missing." He wrapped his arms around her and leaned her against the railing of the widow's walk, so careful not to look out or down, just into her eyes until he kissed her, this time with a little more desperation than ever before.

She shivered in his arms, slack and soft, arching into him as their tongues touched and twirled. When she moaned with pleasure, he lifted her a little, letting her ride him, sliding her up and down until her breath was nothing but helpless gasps. She clung to him, pressing her head into his shoulder, quivering and riding and lost.

With both of them at the hairy edge, he eased her down to the ground, silent, holding her gaze.

"I'll wait as long as I have to," he whispered. "Because you're worth it."

She just closed her eyes and dropped her head against his shoulder. "So are you," she said softly. "Good night."

She slipped away, and he sucked in a breath. "You're just going to leave me up here?"

She held out her hand to him. "I'll help you down, Brock, because I like you so much."

"I like you, too," he whispered. Taking her hand, he headed off the sickeningly high walkway, took her back to her room. There, he kissed her good night and headed to his own room, as disoriented and lost as if he'd stood up on that walkway and jumped.

Chapter Sixteen

For the next week and a half, Brock and Jenna slipped into a pattern that was somehow wonderful and frustrating. The wonderful part was afternoons of "research," which consisted of Brock taking Jenna around to King Harbor businesses so she could talk to employees and townsfolk and watching her piece together a story of a family that Brock couldn't imagine would be anything but flattering.

Nights were wonderful, too, when they shared dinners, walked through town hand in hand or hung out at the Vault. But Jenna kept her promise to hold him at arm's length and, in fact, seemed more determined to go to her room alone every night the deeper she dived into those journals and the past. Oh yeah. That was the frustrating part for Brock. For both of them, really.

But even with all her research, they'd found nothing to explain the money paid to the Platt family, even today, after the long-awaited meeting with an aging lawyer named Bill Whitlock.

He'd been on vacation for almost ten days, but finally came home for Founder's Day. Sadly, the meeting they'd just left with him had delivered up a big bowl of nothing.

"I have never been so frustrated in all my life." Jenna shoved some stray hairs off her face, shooting Brock a look as he revved the Porsche up the driveway toward the estate.

She fluttered through the notes she'd taken during their conversation at Whitlock's house near the harbor. "I mean, how is this possible?" she asked, not for the first time since they'd gotten in his car. "How can no one know anything about seventy-two million dollars? I realize Blackthorne is a big company, but this is a sizable amount."

He saw it differently, though. "Blackthorne has multiple business, all running in the tens of millions in revenue and spending."

"But who loses a million a year?"

"It's not lost," he said. "It went to the Platt Family Trust from my father's personal account, not the business account, and stopped thirteen years ago because Dad's projects were set to continue for seven years after his death."

"Or so Whitlock says." She closed her notebook with a thud. "Shouldn't that lawyer have asked what the money was for?"

"No law says he has to. My father might not have even known. He might have been following instructions from his father."

"Who was covering for *his* father, who stole the recipe."

Brock blew out a breath. "Jenna, you've seen the documentation, the historical records, and the pictures from the original distillery. This whole week while we waited for Whitlock to get back to town, we've talked to every family member and employee—past and present— that you could find. You've grilled Nana until she has to drink six glasses of whisky instead of five. And you've had your head in Meredith's journals every night." He lifted her chin to face him. "Nothing says the recipe was stolen."

"Except a barrel with both their names on it."

He flinched at the memory. "I'm certain that was some weird mistake or even a forgery. Maybe something Platt made to threaten my great-grandfather. There's no record of a connection between the two men anywhere. You even went through all that *King Harbor News* microfiche of articles from ninety years ago. There was nothing."

"Not even an obit for the first Wilfred Platt," she said. "That's just weird."

"Not in the 1930s. Things were different then."

"Not that different that records aren't kept." She turned to him. "What if it *was* blackmail, Brock? What if Alistair wanted something hidden forever?"

"Like the fact that he killed Wilfred?" Even saying the words hurt, but he knew they were both thinking the same thing.

"No, he'd never do a thing like that."

Brock snorted. "You know him so well."

"After reading Meredith's journals, I do. He wasn't capable of murder."

Although Brock knew people were capable of anything. And he supposed stealing a recipe and paying to keep someone quiet beat murdering them and paying to keep them quiet.

"You don't have to worry that I'm going to push that storyline in the book."

He exhaled. "I know you want the truth out, but, man, that would be some clean-up campaign for me." He took her hand and curled his fingers around hers.

"Although I bet it would sell your proposal and I do have a vested interest in that getting done."

She gave a sly smile, letting him know she understood why. "Same, honey."

"Doesn't make it any easier..." He lifted their hands to kiss her knuckles. "To put you in your own room every night."

Her eyes shuttered on a sigh. "Remind me why I wanted to wait for that again."

Laughing, he squeezed her hand. "If I have to remind you, it's a stupid idea."

She turned as they passed Nana's cottage and he caught her nibbling her bottom lip as she stared at the little house. "Stupid to some," she murmured.

"And what if this amazing book does get accepted?" he asked. "I'll still be a...what did you call me? Subject."

She lifted his hand to her lips and placed a kiss on his knuckle. "We'll cross that—"

"Graham's here," he interjected, spotting his uncle's familiar black Range Rover.

"Will I get to talk to him?" She sat straighter, following his gaze. "Even if you're there, Brock, I have to."

"I'm sure you will. He's here for the whole Founder's Day weekend, so there will be time at tonight's cocktail party at the Vault, or even before the parade tomorrow. If you don't have time with him, I will."

"And you'll ask him about Platt and Salmon Falls?"

Maybe. Maybe not. "I can. I can find *something* that can help you write a winning proposal."

"Something...like Claire's secret? Or Alistair's?"

"How else are we going to get this proposal done and accepted?" he said, only half joking.

She narrowed her eyes at him. "So you'd ask him about those things just…for sex?" She laughed a little, but he didn't. He didn't say a word as he climbed out of the car.

She didn't wait for him to open her door, but he met her in front of the car.

"Brock? Would you risk a stain on the Blackthorne name for that?"

He didn't answer for a long time, seriously considering the question as he slid his arms around her and rubbed his hands up and down her back, knowing what he had to say. "If only it was just sex."

He felt the tiny shudder that went through her whole body in response. "It's…not?"

"Is it for you?" he asked.

"There's only been one night of sex…so far."

With a slight smile, he slid his hand along her jawline, thumbing her soft skin. "Every minute that I'm with you, it feels like…" More. So much more. But he couldn't bring himself to say it.

She swallowed, holding his gaze. "It feels like that to me, too," she admitted on a whisper.

"Like what?" he urged, needing her to put into words these feelings he didn't understand or recognize.

"Like…" She smiled. "The opposite of lonely."

"Exactly," he whispered, lowering his head for a kiss.

She reached up and wrapped her arms around his shoulders, gripping hard, pressing into him, opening her mouth to kiss him in a way that always left them both wanting more.

"Hello, Brock."

He froze at the sound of his uncle's voice, slowly inching away from Jenna. Opening his eyes, he looked up to the top step of the porch, where Graham

Blackthorne stood staring at him. Next to him was a much smaller, thinner man Brock didn't recognize.

"Uncle Graham."

With her back to the men, Jenna closed her eyes and let out a nearly silent grunt. To ease the moment of embarrassment for her, he put his arm around her to make the introduction as casual as possible. "I think you've met Jenna Gillespie."

As she turned, he felt her whole body stiffen as she hissed in a shocked breath. The man next to Brock blinked, then his jaw loosened in disbelief. "Jenna?" he asked, his voice gruff with disapproval and disbelief.

"Hello, Mr. Hazlett. What a surprise to see you here."

Hazlett? Her publisher? What the hell was he doing here?

It didn't matter. She'd been caught, and from the look on that man's face, it could cost her everything. One look at Jenna's bloodless face and open mouth confirmed that.

"You look beautiful." Brock delivered the compliment with nothing but sincerity in his dark eyes, reaching out to Jenna when she met him in the great room that evening.

She smiled her thanks, but her gaze shifted around the empty room, as if she expected someone else to jump up from behind the grand piano or step in from the terrace.

"No worries, they've all left for the Vault already. The cocktail party has already started, but we do have to make an appearance."

"I know." She smoothed the white strapless dress she

wore, taking a calming breath. "And...he's going to be there?"

"Ollie? Yes, he'll be there." He eased her closer and planted a kiss on her head, sliding a hand over her bare shoulder. "He told us that this afternoon, or don't you remember?"

The brief conversation in the driveway was a blur. She vaguely recalled Graham Blackthorne explaining that he'd invited Ollie up for Founder's Day weekend, along with some key Blackthorne customers and family friends. After that, she'd begged off to "work," but the only thing she'd done until now was worry that her publisher seeing her sucking face with the main source for the book would be the last nail in the coffin of her already shaky career.

"Did he say anything to you? About...us?"

"Ollie? I didn't talk to him after I left with you," he said, leading her toward the door. "I talked to my uncle, though."

"Did you ask him about Platt and Salmon Falls?"

He snorted. "He wouldn't even dignify that with a response beyond telling me it's stupid, ancient balderdash—that's a quote—that we've dismissed a thousand times." He added some pressure to his hand on her back. "He also urged me to tell you to drop it."

"And if I don't?"

He was silent as they walked down the stairs and he opened his car door for her. Finally, after he got into the driver's seat, he said, "He might have to have a word with Ollie."

The answer hit as hard as if he'd used his fist to deliver it. "He'd get my book killed over it?" She didn't care that her voice rose in anger.

"I don't think it will get to that."

But he didn't know. He didn't know how easily Oliver Hazlett could change her life with the stroke of his pen. It had already happened once.

"The point is you're going in the wrong direction over this. It's not the blockbuster revelation you think it is. There's no *there* there."

Then why was her gut on fire? Why did he refuse to go back to Salmon Falls? Because the barrel with two names on it was too high for him? And why oh why did a Blackthorne give seventy-two million dollars to the Platt family? Her mother would never quit trying to find out, and her father would lose all respect for Jenna if she did.

"So, I'm guessing you didn't get very far asking him about the 'secret' your aunt mentioned before she left."

He groaned softly. "That question wasn't just shot down, it was basically flattened by the verbal machine gun that is Angry Graham."

She shifted in her seat, still torqued about Graham's threat to kill the book. "Maybe I should go to Paris and talk to her."

As he stopped at a light, he turned to her, something so raw and real and unreadable in his eyes, it took her breath away. "Would you do that?"

"I...might. I mean, I could. I should, actually, but maybe not for the proposal. When I write the..." She frowned, searching his face. "Brock, what's wrong?"

He didn't answer until he pulled into the parking lot at the Vault, then he took her hands in his. "Yes," he whispered.

She shook her head, confused. "Excuse me?"

"This afternoon, you asked me if sex with you is worth the risk of...of whatever damage you could do to our family name."

172

"And you want sex so much that it is?"

"I want you," he said. "And I told you, it isn't just sex. I want more than that. I want...*you*, Jenna. Mind, body, and soul."

She sucked in a quick breath at the confession—and the incredible rush of unexpected happiness it gave her. "You're not just saying that to steer me clear of family secrets?"

He looked genuinely hurt that she'd asked. "You do what you have to do," he said. "Dig, talk, ask, travel, whatever. I'm still going to want you. I'm still going to care about you. And I'm still going to wait until this proposal is finished so I can show you how much."

Before she could respond, he leaned in to kiss her hard on the mouth. Pulling her head toward him, he intensified the kiss, melting her into him. She kissed him back, leaning over the console to get more of him, her breath trapped in her lungs, her hands fisted on his chest, her head light and dizzy with need.

"Maybe," she whispered, feeling weak and helpless when his hand landed on her thigh, searing her skin. "We don't have to wait...that long."

He chuckled into the kiss, sliding his hand under the hem of her dress. "Then let's make an appearance at this party and behave like professionals..." His hand traveled higher, hotter with each inch. "So we can get the hell out of here and behave like..." His fingers grazed the lace of her panties. "David and Jenna again."

She moaned into the kiss, all the reasons she had for holding back fading into the background as her entire focus became Brock. "Yes, please."

She was still quivering from the sexy encounter when they walked into the dark, wood-toned, upscale lounge, where a private party was already well underway.

They stayed next to each other, or within eye-contact distance, and every time their fingers brushed or their gazes met, Jenna's whole body weakened like it had in the car. She was sure there was a very good reason not to sleep with Brock Blackthorne, but for the life of her, she couldn't remember it.

Until she turned and came face-to-face with Oliver Hazlett. And just that minute, a woman Jenna recognized as Sarah McKinney, the daughter of the distributor owner negotiating with the Blackthornes, slid her arm around Brock's and stole him away.

"Jenna." Ollie gave her a tight smile. "You seem so surprised to see me."

"I'm delighted to see you," she lied through her own fake smile. "It would have been nice for you to let me know you were coming."

"And miss that lovely display of affection?" He launched a bushy gray brow. "Get your research however you can, right? I'm sure that's what Char May would say."

"I'm sorry, Mr. Hazlett, I fail to see what my mother has to do with this."

He tightened thin lips. "She wouldn't have let the House of Villeneuve debacle happen, for one thing."

Fury skittered down her spine, but she managed to stay perfectly silent.

"So, my dear," he said after an awkward beat. "I do hope all that tonsil hockey is getting you a bombshell, because we will accept nothing less."

"A bombshell?"

"You know, something I couldn't get on the links with Graham. Something deep, dark, dirty, and designed to sell a lot of books."

Like the fact that this whole empire was built on a

recipe Alistair Blackthorne had stolen? Would that be enough? Or did he want blackmail…and murder?

It could all be there if she dug deep enough. She could ruin this family name, and sell a boatload of books, guaranteeing more contracts for her in the future.

"I'm working on it," she said, but even as she spoke the words, they made her feel sick. She didn't want to do that to Brock, or to this family. It'd feel like a betrayal of him and Fiona and even long-dead Meredith.

"It's the Claire thing, right?" Ollie asked after taking a sip and looking past her, already on the hunt for someone more important and exciting. When she didn't answer, his gaze returned to her and narrowed. "You know she left carrying some massive secret. I expect you're finding out what it is."

"I'm looking into…all the history."

He pulled out his phone to read a text, ignoring her for a moment. She glanced around for Brock, but didn't see him anywhere. She did see Sarah McKinney, though, but now she was deep in conversation with Graham, on her tiptoes to talk into his ear over the crowd noise.

"Like that," Ollie said, staring at them. "Are you looking into that relationship? Graham with a beautiful woman practically licking his ear?"

"No, because that woman is part of the McKinney family, which owns a liquor-distribution company that the Blackthornes are negotiating to acquire."

He surreptitiously angled his phone and tapped the screen.

"Did you just take a picture of them?" Jenna asked on a choke.

He shrugged. "I suggest you pursue that line, as well. Graham's infidelity would help your proposal tremendously."

She screwed up her face. "I haven't heard one word about either one of them being unfaithful."

"Really?" He lifted his brows. "Last time we golfed, he had a few drinks and told me he suspected some guy in his boatworks company. Today, he said that was a mistake, but if he's wondering, there must be something to it."

"There's nothing to it," she said with confidence. "I've spent almost two weeks talking to dozens of people in and around this company, and no one has breathed a word of any possible chance either one of them would be unfaithful."

"This picture would say differently." He showed her the phone, and she squinted at the image of Graham with Sarah McKinney whispering in his ear, her hand flat on his chest in a gesture of intimacy that Jenna guessed was anything but. Graham had his arm around her, the camera capturing a split-second expression that could be silly or, to some, sexy.

"Isn't Graham your *friend*?" she asked.

He slipped the phone in his pocket. "So how's your proposal coming along? We'll have it next week, right? I'd love to be able to take it to the editorial board and really push for this to be one helluva profitable project, Jenna."

"Because it's all about the profits, not the story."

He gave her a look that confirmed every word of that. Before she could say anything else, a strong and sure hand landed on her shoulder. "Jenna, I have someone I want you to meet," Brock said. "This man will definitely help with your research."

"Who's that?" Ollie asked.

"Friend of mine named David. Excuse us, will you?" He swooped her away, guiding her through the crowd and slipping into the empty game room. He closed and locked the door behind them, tugging her into darkness.

"David…" she whispered, but the name was trapped by a kiss as he pressed her against the wall. "Mmm. David."

He stroked her sides and breasts, rocking into her, hard and ready. "I can't even talk to people," he confessed. "I can't think about anything but you."

Her knees nearly buckled with each kiss and touch, but he held her pinned to the wall, both of them already moving against each other. "The dart room? You have such bad luck in here."

That made him laugh, but he still managed to work her dress higher. "I'm better at some games than others."

"You're good at…*that*." She could barely breathe it felt so amazing.

He turned. "Pool table or back home?"

She was so damn tempted, but she slid her dress down and found her last shred of common sense. "Take me home, David."

He just smiled and tipped his head to the other side of the room. "There's a back door that only Blackthornes know about." He kissed her again. "There. Now you have a secret. Feel better?"

"I think I'm about to."

Chapter Seventeen

Taking Jenna home was the closest Brock had ever come to driving under the influence. Because he was drunk on the anticipation of getting her into bed, absolutely hammered by the promise of her every time he stopped at a light and they kissed. By the time he parked in the estate drive, his whole body was pulsing with need, and it only got worse when they started kissing again.

"Why do you drive this dumb sports car?" she joked as he trailed kisses down her throat and filled his hand with the sweet curve of her breast.

"Dumb?"

She tried to ease her leg over him. "I can't straddle."

Chuckling at that, he broke the kiss. "Come with me. Plenty of room." He had her out of the car in no time, taking her hand and leading her through a back door, then up to his second-floor suite.

"The attic?" she joked.

"Maybe next time." Outside his door, he pulled her into him and leaned her against the wall again, taking a minute to search her eyes for even the slightest hesitation.

"I'm sure," she whispered as if she'd read his mind.

"What changed? Ollie seeing you here? You figure he knows, so why not?"

"Brock, do you think I make decisions like this based on what my publisher thinks?"

"No, but something changed your mind tonight."

She narrowed her eyes. "I'm tired of making decisions based on the possibility of meeting or missing other people's expectations."

"Good girl."

"The only expectations I want to meet are mine." She smiled. "And yours."

"I don't have any," he said honestly.

"Really?" She reached up and threaded her hands behind his neck, pulling his head toward hers. "Because I'm expecting David to take me into his room, throw me on the bed, and make love until I can't walk to the parade tomorrow."

"Expectations I will meet…and exceed." He kissed her mouth, tasting the remnants of Blackthorne Gold on her lips. He held her around the waist with one hand and opened his bedroom door with the other. There was a light on in the en suite, and some moonlight seeped through the plantation shutters, but the room was mostly shadows.

He knew his way with his eyes closed, though, and he kept them that way as he walked her to the oversize four-poster his aunt had put in the room years after he'd gone to college. He dragged his hands down her sides, settling them on her narrow waist. Then he slowly turned her around to find the zipper of her strapless dress. "Let's start here."

She lifted her hair with two hands in a move that was unfairly sexy, giving him access to a long zipper. Down it went, revealing her bare back, which he had to caress as he unzipped and let the dress fall with a silky whoosh to the floor.

"So long," he whispered, turning her around.

"So long to my dress?"

"I've waited so long for a dress to fall."

Her shoulders moved with a quick laugh. "Not quite two weeks."

"An eternity." He stroked her sides and bare breasts, admiring how she looked in nothing but a snow-white lace thong. "But worth it."

She reached up to unbutton his shirt, and with every open button, she pressed a kiss on his chest while he found new and perfect places to touch.

As each item of clothing hit the ground, his breath grew tighter in his chest. With each touch and kiss and sweet little whimper, his blood rushed faster to the same place. And when they fell onto the bed, naked and ready and hungry for each other, every cell in his body was screaming for Jenna.

Her sighs whispered over him, as warm as her hands and as sweet as her lips. He found new places to kiss, turning her over, lifting her on him, and finally getting her on her back with her hair spilling over his pillow, her eyes closed with raw, unadulterated pleasure.

"Brock, please. Condom. You. Me. *Now.*"

He laughed softly at the somewhat pathetic plea, grabbing the packet from his nightstand and kneeling over her to put it on. While he did, she reached for his hips, still moving hers, biting her lip, groaning with nothing but need.

"Brock," she whispered.

"You mean David." He tossed the empty foil wrapper and settled back down to wrap her sexy thighs around him.

"I mean Brock." Her voice was barely air, but he heard the words and the emotion behind them. "It's Brock I…want."

He found his way into her, sliding slowly, not breathing as the initial blinding rush of pleasure wrapped around his whole body.

"Brock," she said into his mouth, mixing his name with a kiss. "That's who I want. You. Not…some fantasy. You."

He would have responded, but heat and friction took over, stealing his ability to string two words together, unless they were *yes*, *faster*, *more*, and *holy hell, that feels good*.

She arched sharply, her nails digging into his shoulders, her mouth against his skin, the same soft cry he'd heard the first night in the lightning. It pushed them both to the very edge, where he hovered while she lost control and rocked and rolled and clung to him as a climax racked her.

With each stroke, the pressure reached the breaking point, pushing and pulling and building until all he could do was open his eyes, look into hers, and free fall into a long, blinding release that felt like it lasted forever but would never be enough.

Finally, he relaxed onto her, spent and spinning and soaked with sweat.

Only then did Brock realize how entirely different this was than the first time.

As that hit him, he lifted his head, blinking in the dim light to look at her flushed face and sparkling eyes. Yes, she was the same woman he'd essentially hooked up with after an hour in the rain. The same body, hair, eyes, and sweet, sweet voice that he'd left the next morning with a promise for more that night.

Then why was this so different? Why was his heart and head getting in the game that belonged to an entirely different part of his body, in just a matter of a few weeks?

Her eyes opened slowly to look up at him. "Brock?"

That was one difference. He wasn't David, he was Brock. But was that all?

"Everything okay?"

Was it? He let out a ragged breath and lowered himself so their bodies were in full contact again. "I don't know," he whispered, hearing the rough honesty in his voice.

She tried to push his shoulder back to see his face, but he kept his nose nuzzled in her neck and hair, inhaling something that smelled like Nana's garden and moonlight and sex and deep kisses on the widow's walk and lobster rolls and laughter and…oh no.

He was in love with her, that was the difference.

"Brock, what's the matter?"

Nothing. Everything. The world was tilted, and he was…connected to her. And nothing in him wanted that to change. Ever.

"Jenna," he whispered, slowly withdrawing from her body, but knowing that he was still in there, somehow.

"What?"

"You're…" *The only woman I ever want to be with.*

"Yes?"

"I'm…" *Hopelessly gone for you.*

"You're what?"

"That was…" *Way more than just sex.* "Great," he finally managed.

She just laughed and pulled him against her. "It sure was. Rest up for round two, honey."

Okay, maybe for her it wasn't love, but he'd get her there. He knew he would.

Jenna woke with that sudden sharp clarity that usually meant a good idea had been gifted to her in her sleep. Something profound, something memorable, something worth writing about.

Brock.

She closed her eyes again and just let herself enjoy the indescribable comfort of his body curved against her back, the heavy arm tight around her waist, the male hardness pressed against her lower back.

Oh yes, he was profound, memorable, and worthy of every word she could conjure up. Like *dear* and *sexy* and *good* and *wonderful*, and he made her feel…she frowned, rooting for the word.

What *was* the opposite of lonely? Just as whole and complete and finished as a body could be. That's what this man did to her.

There. That. Something…*worth writing about.*

That sense of clarity zipped through her again. A feeling she'd learned long ago not to ignore. A thread of something better than what she thought it could be.

The opposite of lonely.

That was the story of the Blackthornes, she realized with a start, going all the way back to Alistair and Meredith. *That* was their secret. The whole unit—cousins, brothers, aunts, uncles, grandparents, alive and dead—was so integrated that no one could or would ever be lonely when wrapped in the Blackthorne blanket.

She stirred, getting up against her will, needing to get to her laptop and write this concept, already thinking of the very fiber in Brock that made him so proud of being a Blackthorne. It's what made them all proud. It wasn't wealth or whisky or boats or businesses. It was an indescribable sense of *alwaysness* that anyone born to it would feel forever.

"Hey, hey." He tightened his grip and held her in place. "No escape."

"I have to—"

"Okay. Fast. Come right back afterward."

"—write."

He choked a laugh. "Impressive work ethic. Also dumb." He slid his hand over her tummy, then lower. Much, much lower. "This, however…" His clever fingers moved into her. "Is very smart."

Shuddering at his touch, she let him stroke her, but as powerful as the pull for more of him was, her idea was burning. It was pure Char May, really. That's what she did to any subject or topic: She dug until she found the essence and then shone a spotlight on it.

"I need to write."

He just laughed, turning her over. "You need to…oh, yeah, that's your work face. Really? Now?"

She sighed, dragging her hand down to stroke him, sighing at the size and length and pure maleness of him. "I'm afraid you'll make me forget my brilliant idea."

He grunted as she let go of him. "I promise you my idea is more brilliant."

"No, mine is…amazing."

He eased back, his eyes coming into morning focus. "What is it?"

"I kind of want to surprise you, but I think I can finish the proposal now."

He lifted a brow. "You're forgetting who has final approval of whatever you write."

"You can read it when I'm done. But I need some time this morning." She slipped farther away, each inch a little painful as the sheets grew cooler.

"Parade's at noon," he said. "Don't you want to ride the float with all the other Blackthornes?"

"Your family rides? I thought it was just some distillery and boatworks employees."

"For the first part of the parade, we've always been on the float, ever since I was little. Kind of a show of family solidarity."

She smiled, knowing she'd put that in her proposal. "I'd love to, but how much time do I have?"

He rolled over and picked up his phone to check the time, then frowned. "What the hell?" After a moment, he sat up, the scowl deepening as he brought the phone closer. "What the holy freaking *hell*?"

"What's the matter?"

For a moment, he didn't say anything, staring at the phone and making her ache to lean over and look at the screen, but the dismay—maybe fury—rolling off him held her back.

"Did you know he was going to do this?"

"Know…what? Who?"

Finally, he turned the phone to her, showing her what looked like a screenshot of an Instagram post, the picture suddenly extremely familiar. "Ollie took that," she whispered, feeling a sick sensation in her belly.

"He might have, but you got the photo credit." He pushed the phone a little closer so she could read the fine print on the Instagram account of the tabloid *Celebrity Watch*.

Celebrity biographer and daughter of superstar Char May, Jenna May Gillespie, teases readers with this photo taken as she conducts research for a shocking exposé of the Blackthornes, one of America's wealthiest and most fascinating families. Recently separated from his wife, who has relocated to France in the wake of her own rumored affair, family patriarch and company CEO Graham Blackthorne is shown here with his latest conquest, the daughter of a major liquor distributor being acquired by Blackthorne Enterprises. Look for ON THE ROCKS, *the can't-miss insider's view of the destruction that whisky, wealth, and women has brought to this family. Coming next year from Filmore & Fine.*

She just stared at the words, biting back the bile that rose in her throat.

"Brock…this is utter garbage. The title, the picture, the caption, everything."

He tapped the screen of his phone to reveal a string of texts she assumed were from his family.

Silent, he read the texts, then finally looked at her with nothing less than anguish in his eyes. "The McKinneys are talking about canceling the deal, four retailers closed their purchase orders, Devlin just lost a boat contract, and *Imbibe Magazine* just reposted this picture to ten thousand industry followers."

"Oh, Brock. I'm so sorry." She pulled the sheet up, suddenly aware of how exposed she was.

"I just hope my aunt doesn't see this."

"Ollie has to take that down, now. Let's go find him and—"

"He's staying at the Bickmore Hotel and you might want to check in, too."

She froze. "Excuse me?"

"Graham has asked that you leave, immediately." He climbed out of bed on the other side, grabbing a pair of sweats hanging over a chair. "We're meeting in a few minutes to prepare a response and launch damage control before this gets any—"

"Brock, you can't possibly blame me for this. You know I didn't post it. You know none of that is true. You know…" She fisted the sheet at her chest, watching him move with precision and…ice. "You do blame me."

"I blame myself," he muttered. "I should have been more vigilant in protecting the family name. But if you can put some pressure on your buddy Ollie to get that taken down, it could help my family."

My family. For reasons she didn't understand, those two words cut her heart more than anything else. No, they didn't cut her heart…they cut her out.

He pulled on a T-shirt and strode to the door, turning. "I have to go, Jenna. I'm…sad this has to end like this."

"This…this morning or this relationship? What *this* are you talking about?"

"Look, I…I gotta fix this."

He slipped out the door, closing it behind him and leaving her speechless and heartbroken. "No, Brock," she whispered, sliding out of bed. "You have to fix this. Me. Us."

But then, deep inside, she'd always known there wasn't an *us* in her future—not with Brock, not with anyone. She didn't know what the opposite of lonely was, and the truth was, she might never.

Chapter Eighteen

The weather didn't look too promising for the big parade. But overcast skies were the least of Jenna's problems. Right now, all she could think about was finding Ollie and demanding he take care of the situation.

The Bickmore Hotel was on the parade route, so the crowded lobby didn't surprise Jenna when she walked in later that morning. All of the antique settees were full, and large groups peppered the gleaming hardwood floors of King Harbor's upscale hotel. Would Ollie be down here, or would they ring his room for her?

Didn't matter. If Jenna had to steal a maid's uniform and knock on every door, she would. Of course, he'd ignored her calls, and his office was closed on a Saturday. But Jenna wasn't going to let this go.

First, she was going to get that picture taken down. Then, she was going to call her agent and get out of this contract. And after all that, she'd find a way to prove to Brock that she had nothing but respect for his family. If she lost him, well, so be it. That would hurt. But she wouldn't slink away without fixing the mess.

She scanned the lobby again, casing the three clerks to decide which might be the most likely to give her the room number of a guest. None, probably. Then she glanced at a bearded man in camo pants and a T-shirt walking toward the elevators and sucked in a shocked breath.

What the heck was Roger Platt doing here?

Without a second's hesitation, she strode over to him, not sure how she expected him to react to seeing her here.

"Oh, I found you," he exclaimed.

She sure hadn't expected *that*. "You were looking for me?"

"Have been for a few days, but I never got your name, and I didn't have the nerve or desire to hunt down a Blackthorne."

"What are you doing here?"

"I called that book company you mentioned. Filmore? After six different people talked to me, I finally got through to a guy named…"

When he frowned, Jenna finished for him. "Oliver Hazlett."

"Yeah. And I told him I needed to talk to you."

Oliver never mentioned that last night, Jenna thought. Whatever Roger had, Oliver was going to take it and…do what with it? Make sure it sold books, the way salacious pictures did on Instagram? "Well, here I am. What do you need?"

He looked from one side to the other, and she automatically guided him to an empty seat under a window. "Here. Let's talk."

When they sat down, he stared at her, looking hard at her face.

"Yes?" she urged.

"After you left, I was pissed. And wanted to know why the hell we got mystery money for so long that the

Platt family became pretty stupidly rich, but then it stopped."

"I want to know, too."

"So I went digging into the graves."

She recoiled at that, but stayed silent.

"There ain't no dead people there," he said. "It's where my granddad started keeping the money since he hated banks. Anyway, one of 'em was the first one my granddad dug, and he was the only one allowed to dig there. My grandma said you'd die if you tried, so no one ever did. Until you came, and then I decided to dig, and I found…"

"Money?"

He shook his head. "These." He reached into his pocket and pulled out a small white envelope, opening it and dumping something into his hand.

She leaned closer to see gold cufflinks with yellowish stones. "What are they?"

"Human teeth."

She jerked back with a gasp. "What?"

"I heard it was a mob thing during Prohibition. Al Capone started it. Like a trophy for a kill."

Her heart slammed as she took another quick look at his palm. "And…"

"And this was in the jar with them." He pulled a card out of the envelope and handed it to her. The front was embossed in gold with nothing but one name: *Augustino Satrielli.*

"Who is that?"

"Turn it over."

She did and read the tiny handwritten words.

W — Unless you want my next pair to be made of Alistair Blackthorne's teeth, put the money and the recipe in the barrel that has both your names on it. You can save that son of a bitch. Or I can get new jewelry.

She looked up at him. "Maybe your great-grandfather saved Alistair's life." And maybe *that's* why he paid the family seventy-two million dollars.

He shrugged and closed his fingers around the disgusting tooth jewelry. "'Cept I looked through every barrel we ever had at our place. Ain't no barrel with both their names on it."

Oh yes, there was.

For a long moment, she said nothing. Was it possible that something in that barrel they'd spotted in the distillery could remove any stain on the Blackthorne name? Maybe even polish it up, if Alistair had done something that good for the other family? At the very least, maybe Augustino left the recipe in there.

"Thank you, Roger."

He stood up and shoved his hands and treasures into his pockets. "It's a lot of money, and none of the living Platts know why we used to get it. We want to."

"So do I." As she stood, she stared at Roger for a long time, trying to decide if she'd rather have Ollie's room number so she could march up there to demand he get that picture taken down...or head back to that distillery to possibly get her hands on the best-kept secret in Blackthorne history. One that would show the world one of the many reasons they had a right to be proud.

Seriously, it was no contest.

By the time the meeting broke up, it was pouring, and the dark skies were a perfect match for Brock's mood. He'd taken enough shit from Graham and Trey to last a lifetime in the past few hours, but among them all—since Logan, Phillip, and Devlin joined them—they were able to get on the phone to put out a few fires and hold off some others. To his credit, Trey saved the McKinney deal with some very smooth talking and a few new promises on the negotiating table, and Devlin recouped the boat order.

But it was up to Brock to get the photo taken down and get a retraction, so he was going to have to go into town and hunt down that son of a bitch Hazlett, unless Jenna had already succeeded there. At the moment, the picture was still up and gathering comments.

"Parade's been postponed for a few hours due to weather," Logan said, pulling out his phone to read it as they walked out of Graham's office and headed through the oversize kitchen of the estate. "Better hope Hazlett hasn't left town early."

"I'll find him, but first I want to find Jenna." And apologize for being an ass. Unless she was already—

"She's gone." Nana popped her head out from behind a newspaper, where she was tucked away at the kitchen table.

His blood went cold at the announcement. She'd really left? He'd hoped she would ignore that unfair order, but now...

"In the Range Rover, a while ago," Nana said.

Relief washed over him as he slid out his phone and called her. "Then she's not gone for good."

Logan threw him a look. "I sure hope to hell you didn't tell her that my dad said she should leave. He was just pissed as hell."

"I..." *Am an idiot.* "I know where she went," he said, stepping toward the door, listening to the phone until his call went to voice mail. "I'll find her."

On the short drive to the Bickmore, Brock peered

through the windshield wipers and rain for any sign of the estate Range Rover, swiping his hair back and blowing out noisy exhales of frustration.

He should never have left her like that, never let her think he blamed her for something out of her control. He'd explained that in the family meeting, but his words had fallen on deaf ears. His family members were more concerned about undoing the damage to the business than exactly how it happened.

With no sign of the Range Rover in the hotel parking lot, he left his car with the valet and rushed into the elegant hotel lobby, marching straight to the counter to demand they call Oliver Hazlett. But that wasn't necessary, because he recognized one of the desk clerks from the Vault.

She gave him a bright smile, and he returned it, dismissing any guilt if she thought he was flirting, because after a two-minute conversation, he was in the elevator, heading to room 546.

No one answered the first knock, but when he called Hazlett's name, the door opened slowly to reveal the little man with wire-rimmed glasses and narrowed, distrustful eyes.

"Mr. Black—"

"Get it down," he said through gritted teeth.

Hazlett paled. "I'm sure I don't know—"

"Yes, you do. Get that rag to take down the picture and issue a complete retraction *now*."

He swallowed. "I can make a call." When he tried to close the door, Brock blocked it with his foot. "I'll listen to the conversation."

To his credit, Hazlett didn't try to fight Brock, but let him into the entry hall, where a suitcase was packed and ready to roll.

Silent, Hazlett pulled out a cell phone and tapped the screen, then put the phone to his ear.

"On speaker," Brock demanded.

His eyes shuttered in frustration, but he did as he was told. A moment later, a voice mail message for John Germaine of *Celebrity Watch* came through the speaker.

"Hey, John, Ollie Hazlett here. I was, uh, wondering if you could do me a favor and pull that Insta post about the Blackthorne book? It turns out the source was wrong. So, uh, I know you don't want misinformation floating around. Let me know when you can pull it. Okay, thanks." He tapped the phone and gave a tight smile. "Good?"

"Far from it," Brock said. "Why would you feed that crap to a tabloid? Just to sell books? To put Jenna in a corner? To ruin her relationship with..." *Me.* "The family?"

He snorted, setting the phone on top of the suitcase. "I'll take door number one: to sell books, sir. Surely you understand that."

On the suitcase, Hazlett's phone rang.

"Answer it," Brock said. "I want proof that picture's coming down."

Without taking his eyes from Brock, he reached down and touched the phone screen.

"Hey, it's Roger Platt."

Roger Platt? Brock's stomach tightened as the name echoed through the room. What the ever-lovin' hell was he doing on the phone?

"I can't wait much longer for you, Mr. Platt," Hazlett said. "I have a plane to catch."

"Then catch it," he said. "I saw that lady writer in the lobby and told her what I needed to tell you."

"Which is what?" Brock demanded.

At the sound of another man's voice, Platt went silent for a few seconds. Then the phone clicked off.

"What the hell was that all about?" Brock fisted his hands, ready to wring the skinny guy's neck if he didn't get a straight answer.

"One of Jenna's sources wanted to give me information for her since she's been so...unavailable." His brows flickered. "I do wonder how long she's just going to ride her mother's fame."

"So you haven't seen her?" he asked.

"Not since you two left the party unconscionably early."

Then the only person she'd talked to was Platt. And she hadn't checked in to the hotels, as he'd so horribly suggested. The girl at the front desk confirmed that. So, where was she?

Without another word, Brock stepped back into the hall and as he walked, tried to call Jenna. Once again, the call went to voice mail.

Frustrated, he headed back down to the lobby then out to the street, coming to a complete stop when he was soaked by pouring rain and a flash of lightning.

All he could think was that Jenna was alone in a storm and needed him.

Chapter Nineteen

A little lightning. That's all it was. A flash here, a rumble there.

Jenna gripped the leather-wrapped steering wheel of the Range Rover, refusing to let the weather deter her as she found her way back to the Salmon Falls Distillery. It wasn't listed as a location on her GPS, but the actual falls were, and once there, she was sure this four-wheel-drive beast could get her through the route they'd followed on foot.

The entire trip, she'd banged out a plan in her head for getting safely up into the loft. First, she stopped at the hardware store and bought a small grappling hook and rope, two powerful flashlights, and a Swiss Army knife. Then she visualized how to create a barrel pyramid to get her higher than Brock had been when he'd tried to get up there. And she'd have her phone to call him if she needed help.

But right now, she just wanted to find whatever might be left in the barrel with two names, then surprise him with what she found. Not only did she want to prove to him she was on the Blackthornes' side, but whatever she wrote about them would *not* be for Filmore & Fine.

Damn Ollie and his quest for profits.

The rain intensified as she got closer to the falls, but she managed to spot a side road she remembered them taking that day. Turning onto it, she moved on instinct and memory, eventually rolling up to the dilapidated distillery, sitting in the car for a moment to let her heart rate, and maybe the rain, slow.

Neither did.

After a few minutes, she gathered her bag of tools, said a silent prayer, waited out the next bolt of lightning and thunder, then made a dash. With every step, she held her breath in fear until she reached the sliding door that Brock had shown her the last time they were there.

Inside, the building seemed bigger, darker, and even creepier than that last visit. She stood for a minute in the main, open area, flinching at a bolt of lightning flashing outside the missing windows.

The sooner she got in and out, the better.

She headed to the stairs to the basement, using one of the flashlights to light her way. The stairs weren't nearly as steep as she remembered, but then, she and Brock hadn't had a light. This time, she could easily see where she was going, but that might not have been a good thing. The basement was filthy, dank, and right out of a horror movie.

Rain splattered down one wall, turning it black and dripping loudly at the bottom. The barrel that Brock had used to climb was right where he'd left it, though. And so was the barrel with two names on it, up high in the loft. Was the proof she needed in there?

As she made her way across the basement, she shone the light on the spot where they'd been sitting, with the unopened bottle of whisky right where they'd left it, tempting her with its liquid courage.

But she ignored it all and moved the beam up to the loft, holding it on that barrel.

Jenna moved on instinct and hope, wrapping some rope around her waist and knotting it, then tying the grappling hook to the end. She'd never climbed a mountain in her life, but the approach made sense and seemed safe...*ish*.

Starting to sweat, she created her pyramid of barrels, two on the bottom and one on top of that. It took her about seven feet off the ground so she could just about reach the bottom rung of the makeshift ladder of two-by-fours. With her phone in her pocket, two flashlights on the floor aimed up to light her way, she started to climb.

Outside, thunder rumbled nearly constantly, close by and in the distance. With her full concentration on her task, she ignored it. It wasn't until she had her hands on the wall-mounted rungs that she realized this was the first time in memory that she'd lived through a storm and hadn't yet thought of that awful day in the closet.

If nothing else, that made this venture worth the trouble.

She climbed to the next rung. So far, so good. She was able to climb past the board that had broken under Brock's weight, getting a kick of satisfaction as she got higher.

A clap of thunder almost made her lose her grip on the board for a split second, but she held tight and finally got to the loft, which smelled like mold and dust and... whisky. Was there whisky in that barrel? No money and no recipe?

Time to find out.

"Please don't break," she whispered as she put some pressure on the first floorboard of the loft. When it held, she added some more pressure, and more, and then took her little hook and smacked it into a solid piece of wood for insurance before she climbed up into the loft.

The floor squeaked, sagged an inch, but it held her.

Moving gingerly, she crawled the few feet to the barrel, taking out her phone to add more light.

The now familiar barrel-and-thistle logo was crystal clear up close, burned into the oak, along with the words *Platt Blackthorne Distilleries. Contents: Platt Gold Whiskey.*

Careful not to release her safety grappling hook, she stood slowly and pulled out the Swiss Army knife, praying like hell this didn't end up covering her in a barrel full of hundred-year-old liquid gold.

She stabbed the seam on the top like she'd seen Brock do during their tour of the distillery, forcing the knife into the crack. Then she wiggled, sliced, and twisted until she heard a *pop.*

Very, very carefully, she lifted the lid, bracing for the onslaught of whisky smells, but there was nothing but…a little dust.

Her heart pounding, she took her phone and shone the light inside, gasping out loud at the gun resting at the bottom.

"Holy…" She stared at it, blinking at the revolver, almost afraid to touch it. No, definitely afraid to touch it. "What the hell?"

She squinted, seeing that it rested on a white piece of paper. The recipe? She wanted to reach in, but didn't want to bump a revolver that might or might not be cocked…or maybe have someone's fingerprints on it.

Taking a deep breath and holding it, she reached all the way in and grazed the edge of the paper, just barely managing to get it between her fingertips and slide it out ever so slowly so she didn't disturb that gun.

Letting that breath out, she directed the light on the paper and stared at the words written in the same hand she'd seen on that card.

To Whom It May Concern:
Let it be known to anyone who finds the body of Alistair Blackthorne that he deserved to die. When you cross the powers that be, you meet the wrong end of our gun. And if you made it this far, you won't be alive for long. We made sure of that.
Augie "The Duke" Satrielli

The Duke? The man Meredith Blackthorne wrote she was scared of meeting? But the mafia didn't kill Alistair Blackthorne. Fiona told her Alistair died at the ripe old age of ninety-five and was buried at the estate. But The Duke must have thought he killed Alistair...

They ain't never found his body.

She was right. The mafia mistakenly killed Wilfred Platt, and that had to be the reason Alistair had arranged to pay a million dollars a year to the Platt family. It had nothing to do with a stolen recipe. It was guilt for the wrong man taking the mafia's bullet. It was an act of caring for the Platt family.

She had to get down. She had to call Brock and—

The board under her shifted with a noisy crack. Gasping, she rolled off of it just as the wood split from the piece next to it, falling twenty feet with a noisy thud.

"Oh God." She flailed for a second, and the next board sagged suddenly, creaking under her like a whine of warning that it was next. On a shriek, she shoved herself farther toward the wall, bumping into another barrel that was leaning at an odd angle. It rocked, rolled, and fell, tumbling all the way down and exploding with a crash of splintered wood and…whisky.

You won't be alive for long. We made sure of that.

By booby-trapping the boards?

The smell wafted up, making her slam a hand over her mouth and nose and turn away toward the wall, where she saw something behind the remaining barrel. It was round and white and smooth with holes and—

She screamed so hard the vibrations ripped at her throat, a shout of terror so real and raw that nothing could silence her as she stared at the skull. And bones. A full skeleton lying right next to her in an abandoned basement during a thunderstorm.

Just as her scream turned into a sob of horror, the last board cracked, making her slide down, grabbing helplessly at the broken wood. The Platt Blackthorne barrel fell past her, landing with a crack and the deafening pop of a single bullet being fired.

Her board didn't break, but her grappling hook slipped free, hanging from her body toward the ground. She clung to the last piece of wood nailed to the wall, dangling twenty feet above hard concrete.

If she lost her grip or the board broke, she would die in a pool of whisky.

All roads led to Roger Platt. They might be muddy, washed out, and difficult to find, but Brock moved on instinct and that old gut feeling that used to spur him on during a lively game of hide-and-seek. Psych out the person you're looking for, think of the most obvious place they'd be, then go somewhere slightly different but still the same.

This time-tested formula took him to Salmon Falls, but as he neared the home of Roger Platt, he veered off in a different direction. Too obvious, too simple.

Gut instinct was sending him to the distillery. The barrel. The heart of this.

A spidery white line zipped through the slate-gray sky, followed almost immediately by a clap of thunder. With each one of those, his heart cracked a little more, and he drove a little faster, imagining Jenna braving the storm to get to the truth. The thunder still echoed as he neared the distillery, coming around the last bend to see...

The Range Rover.

"Thank God," he muttered, throwing the Porsche into park and whipping open the door with no regard for the rain. His foot hit mud, but he sloshed to the other car, squinting inside. But any hopes that she might be sitting out the storm were dashed.

No, she'd gone after that barrel, twenty-some feet in the air.

He ran full speed to the entrance, which had been left open. Just as he opened his mouth to call her name, he heard a long, muffled, blood-curdling scream almost immediately followed by the deafening pop of a gunshot.

"Jenna!" He croaked her name, breaking into a run across the floor toward the basement, forcing himself not to call out again in case someone was down there with a gun.

He paused for one second at the top of the stairs, blinking at the strange uplighting, listening and hearing...a low moan and whimper, followed by fast, short breaths.

Without making a noise, he headed down, coming to the bottom to see Jenna clinging to the last board of the loft, dangling high over the concrete floor covered with whisky.

Once again, he kept from calling out, because scaring her with a loud shout might make her fall.

"Jenna." He almost whispered the word. "Don't move. I'm here. I'm going to save you."

"Brock," she sobbed.

"Please don't move." He started across the basement, looking up, trying to imagine how the hell she got all the way up there.

"There's…a dead man…up here."

"Did you shoot him?"

"Someone did. Eighty-some years ago."

Ooof. "Okay." His feet splashed in what had to be a barrel's worth of whisky on the floor. "Let's just make sure there isn't a dead woman down here."

"Mmm."

She was trying hard not to cry, her arms quivering, her legs dangling, her whole body facing away so he couldn't see her face. But he didn't want to distract her or take one more second than necessary.

"There's a hook," she rasped. "If you throw it and hit the wood, it might hold me."

And it might not, but it would be added insurance if he dropped her when she fell. "Okay, okay. I have it." He closed his fingers over the grappling hook. "I'm going to throw it."

"Aim for the wood."

Aim. Like darts. Oh *man*. "Okay." He grabbed the hook, closed one eye, spotted his target, and reached his arm back. He could do this. He had to do this. "Here it comes."

He whipped the hook into the air, watching it arc past her, and…*thwap*. It hit the wood and held.

"Oh, good," she managed. "Now what?"

If she just let go, he might catch her, but the fall was so far, it could hurt them both. It could kill her. He had to get her himself. He had to climb *all the way* up there. *Shit.*

"Just hang on one more minute, babe," he said as he eyed the barrels she'd stacked. Would that work? Maybe.

He pushed up onto the first one, got his balance, then climbed onto the one in the middle, wobbling a little just as a loud roll of thunder echoed upstairs. Gritting his teeth, he found his footing on the first rung of the makeshift ladder, grabbing the strip of wood right above his head. He took one step.

One down, seven more to go…and then he had to grab her and bring her down without falling.

"Brock." She whispered his name, and he looked up to see she'd turned slightly to watch him. "Are you sure? Can you do it?"

"For you?" He gave her a tight smile. "I can do anything."

She sighed softly. "Keep your eyes on me. Not the ground."

He took the next one, then the next, then the next, holding her gaze every moment, getting closer, refusing to look down. Finally, he reached what was left of the loft and gauged how far he had to reach, stretching out his arm toward her and missing by six inches.

"You'll have to let go with one hand and reach for me," he told her.

"Can you hold both of us?"

"I don't know," he said honestly. "But we don't have a choice."

For a long moment, she said nothing, but the wood she clung to creaked.

"Jenna, you have seconds before the decision is made for you. Reach out, and I'll catch you." He kept his voice steady and calm, the opposite of everything he felt in his body.

"I…can't."

"Sure you can," he said gently, coaxing her closer. "I'm right here for you. I'm here."

Her only answer was a soft sob, a tear rolling down her cheek. "I'm so scared, Brock."

"I'm going to catch you, and hold you, and never let you go." He took a breath, reaching out to her. "You're never going to be lonely again," he said softly. "You know why, right? You know I'm falling in love with you. So you're going to fall right back."

"Mmm. Poetic. And crazy."

"I am. About you. And nothing's going to change that. So you have to trust me and take my hand. Trust me to hold you and love you…forever."

"Brock…"

"Let go, babe. Let go."

He saw it hit her, saw the very second she trusted him. Her arms loosened, her feet relaxed. She took a deep breath, let it out, and released her grip, closing one hand around his.

He looked at their joined hands, but accidentally got a glimpse of the ground, which looked like it was a thousand miles away. Bile rose in his throat, and blood pumped noisily in his head, and he damn near let go of the board he clung to.

"Brock. Look at me."

He did. "I got you," he assured her. "Now, Jenna. Now."

She let go completely, her weight tugging him down, but he gripped the board with his right hand and every ounce of strength he had. "Wrap yourself around me."

She hugged him with her arms and legs, clinging as he shifted all of their weight down one treacherous step after another, finally putting his feet on the top barrel. It wobbled from one side to the other, but he fought for control and released her when he had it.

Standing on top of that pyramid of oak, they wrapped their arms around each other and finally let out the longest breaths of relief.

He kissed her hair and held her tight. "I love you, Jenna."

Without waiting for a response, he slowly released her, stepped down to the first barrel, then jumped to the floor, coming around to look up at her face. "Now you can get down."

She just nodded, sitting, then guiding herself to the bottom barrel, where he scooped her into his arms and pulled her against his chest.

Neither said a word while they stood ankle-deep in whisky, clinging to each other as they caught their breath and let their heart rates slow.

Finally, she inched back, her tearstained face looking so much like the first night he'd found her in another storm.

"I love you, too," she whispered. "And, wow, do I have a story to tell."

Chapter Twenty

"Here." Fiona stuck a glass nearly full of whisky into Jenna's hand. "You need this more than I do."

"I will not say no." Jenna took the glass and put her other arm around the tiny woman, who'd been like a rock for what felt like a lifetime of intense questioning by the local police and then the FBI agents who'd swooped into the estate. But it might have been only a few hours—Jenna had been cooped up in the library answering questions for what seemed like hours, on top of all the time they'd spent at the distillery when the authorities showed up.

"What time is it?" she asked, still feeling disoriented from the entire ordeal and the aftermath.

"Almost ten," Fiona answered. "Everyone is waiting for you in the great room now that the last of those handsome FBI men are gone." She added a soft whistle. "They didn't make cops like that in my day."

"I didn't notice," Jenna said, taking a welcome sip of the silky smooth whisky.

"Because love is blind, and if you even try to tell me…" Fiona lifted a brow, making Jenna laugh.

"Come on, I'll face the Blackthornes."

"Face them? They are the ones who have to face you. And thank you. Of course, Brock's waiting impatiently for you. Oh, Jason and Mallory flew in from Los Angeles on a private plane when all the hoopla broke." Nana gave her squeeze. "I love a full house, so I have you to thank for that, too."

She walked with Nana to the great room, scanning the room full of mostly familiar faces. Instantly, Brock broke from a close conversation with Graham, Trey, and Logan to greet her with a simple hug.

Phillip sat close to Ashley on a sofa, across from Devlin, standing behind Hannah, who sat in an oversize chair. Across the room was a handsome man who looked enough like the rest of the Blackthornes for her to guess he was Brock's brother Jason, with his girlfriend, Mallory.

"Ladies and gentlemen," Brock said in a loud, dramatic voice, quieting the room. "Let's hear it for the woman of the hour. This lady has single-handedly dispelled a myth that was an albatross around the neck of the Blackthorne name for decades. And she unearthed a story of our past that proves our ancestor Alistair Blackthorne not only didn't steal the recipe for Blackthorne Gold, but he paid the family that first grew the sugar gold corn needed to make it and then arranged for that very family to be taken care of after his partner took a bullet meant for him."

A loud cheer erupted, along with some noisy claps, hoots, hollers, and a kiss from Brock right on the lips.

"And she risked her life to do it." Graham Blackthorne took a few steps closer, his gaze pinned on Jenna. "We are all indebted to you," he said.

"No, no. I didn't do anything but..." She looked up at Brock. "Are they sure that's exactly what happened? The last FBI agent I talked to just asked questions and didn't give me any answers to mine."

Brock laughed. "I bet you loved that."

"Not too much," she admitted.

"The disappearance of Wilfred Platt had been a cold case since 1934," Brock said. "They suspected it was tied to the mafia as things got desperate right before Prohibition ended."

"And if that body is Wilfred?" she asked.

Brock nodded. "They'll do DNA, but it's him. Now they have proof that he was killed by Augie Satrielli, one of New England's most infamous mobsters of the era. They got Augie on other charges, so he did his time, and an old confession confirmed that the mob was siphoning cash from Platts and Blackthornes. So, we're guessing Wilfred went to talk to them and they killed him, either thinking he was Alistair or not caring that he wasn't."

"Either way, your great-grandfather felt guilty and that's why he paid the Platt family." Jenna let out a sigh, relieved the reason for the payments was much more noble than blackmail.

On her other side, Fiona slipped her arm around Jenna. "We've all acted like we didn't believe the old rumors," she said. "But I've always worried and wondered if our fortunes were born on the backs of others. My heart is so light to know that my father-in-law was actually, at one time, partners and friends with Wilfred Platt, not a competitor."

Trey stepped forward, looking as sharp as if this were a nine a.m. meeting in his office. "We're going to start using Platt's sugar gold corn exclusively for our King Harbor Distillery," he said. "And we'll resume the payments indefinitely. I've already been in touch with Roger Platt."

"And…" She glanced around. "Ollie Hazlett is gone?"

"For good," Graham announced. "I've been on the phone with a few members of the Filmore & Fine board of directors, who can't apologize enough for the incident with the photograph."

Brock added a squeeze to her shoulders. "No question your book proposal will be approved, whatever you decide to write."

She smiled up at him, remembering the brief conversation they'd had while waiting for the cops to arrive at the distillery. After a moment, she looked around at the room, feeling a connection to this family already.

She cared about them, even the ones who weren't here, like Brock's aunt. But she felt certain that, knowing how the Blackthornes worked, someone would persuade Claire to come home soon. Maybe even Graham himself, who looked just a little bit lost in the room full of so many happy couples.

"I do want to write a book about this family," she finally said. "But I want to do it on my terms, and write the story I want to tell."

Any chatter in the room died down as she talked. "I want to tell the story of Alistair and Meredith Blackthorne," she said. "They are fascinating. The bedrock of this family, the founders of greatness, and they were madly in love with each other until the day they died."

Another cheer and lots of toasts to that.

"Then Filmore & Fine can publish that book," Nana said.

"Or I can do it myself," Jenna replied.

"Oh, hell, yes you can," Brock said. "This woman can do anything."

As the laughter quieted, the man Jenna assumed was Jason stepped forward and extended his hand. "And I'll buy the movie rights," he said as he shook Jenna's hand. "I'm Brock's brother, Jason," he said.

"Oh, hello," Jenna said warmly. "I've heard so much about you."

"No doubt you heard I'm the rebel Hollywood guy in the family tree." He had the dark good looks of a Blackthorne, for sure, but also had a laid-back energy that didn't seem to belong in this family. "But I'd honestly love to bring Alistair and Meredith's story to the screen."

She pressed her knuckles to her chest. "A movie?" Now there was something neither of her parents had ever done. She could hear Char May's exclamations already.

"Pretty sure that's why Brock convinced Mallory and me to fly out here today from LA, and I'm glad he did." He gestured toward a beautiful woman with short, tousled blond hair and thick black glasses, who came closer to be introduced.

About six different conversations started at once, with laughter and more toasts, but Jenna just turned to Brock and lifted her glass. "I told you there is nothing boring, ordinary, or unremarkable about this family," she whispered with a tease in her voice.

"Take a drink," he volleyed back, tapping his glass to hers.

She laughed as Logan came up next to her. "Does this mean we'll be seeing more of you in Boston, Jenna?"

"I..." She looked up at Brock, who just beamed at her. "Yes, I think I'll be writing that book in Boston."

Brock tightened his grip, pulling her a little closer. "From my apartment, I hope."

"Don't tell me, it's a penthouse," Jenna guessed.

"A penthouse?" Logan barked a laugh. "Second floor is as high as this dude gets."

Brock gave her a look that easily communicated their shared secret. "Maybe I could go higher," he said, planting a kiss on her head. "For a good cause."

"Let's hit the Vault." Phillip approached them and put a hand on Brock's back. "I feel like kicking your ass in darts."

Brock just lifted a brow. "Be careful what you wish for, big brother. My aim has improved."

"You just have a great partner."

He laughed and hugged her one more time. "You can say that again."

They left in one big group of brothers, cousins, and girlfriends, piling into cars and slipping into familiar roles. As they laughed and teased and planned for the future, Jenna could feel herself folded into the arms of the man she loved and the great big family that she'd always dreamed of having.

Epilogue

"Oh my gosh, I cannot get used to that blinding sunshine." Karen strode into Brock's office, squinting at the light that poured through his floor-to-ceiling windows high above Boston. He hadn't closed the shades since he and Jenna had come back from Maine.

"Future's so bright, you gotta wear shades," he joked, dropping the last of the day's work in his out-basket. "And that's it for me today."

Karen looked stunned. "Is it the End Times? You're leaving three hours early?"

"Jenna's flight lands in a few hours, and I'm going home to get my—our—apartment ready so she feels welcome when the movers come with her stuff tomorrow."

Karen's smile faltered. "How long do you think you'll live together?"

"A long time. Why?"

She shrugged. "I just thought, you know…it would be nice or even *better* if you…"

He just laughed. "No worries, Saint Karen. I'm hoping we can set a date for early next year, after we close on the Salmon Falls Distillery and get the refurbishing plans finalized."

"I still can't believe you're buying that old abandoned building that had a dead man in it for nearly ninety years."

"You want to know what else you won't believe? That Roger Platt's going to fire up the old stills, and we're going to make Platt Blackthorne Gold from there." He shook his head. "Alistair would be proud."

"I'm proud," Karen said. "And will be even prouder when the babies start popping."

He almost rolled his eyes, but the fact was, he and Jenna both wanted a big family. "And then I'll be leaving at five on most days. Little League and dance recitals, you know." He chuckled as he slipped on his jacket, but his smile faded when he noticed her eyes had grown misty. "Hey, don't go all soft on me now."

But she pressed her hands together and sighed. "God is so good to answer my prayers."

"Then ask the Big Man to get her flight here on time. I miss that woman. See you tomorrow. Maybe."

A few minutes later, he stepped out to Clarendon Street just as Hoyt pulled up in the stretch limo. So Graham must have scored the town car again. No worries. Jenna would like to be picked up at the airport in this car. They always had fun in the back seat of any car.

"I got it." He signaled to Hoyt to save the man the trouble of getting out. As he opened his door, the smile he wore just grew bigger at the sight of one beautiful blonde in the back seat. "Whoa. Wasn't expecting you."

"You can get in," Jenna said, patting the leather. "If you're not a serial killer."

Laughing, he slid in next to her. "I'm not anything but...insanely happy to see you."

"I got an earlier flight." She leaned into the kiss he offered, and he instantly pulled her closer for more.

Without asking, Hoyt raised the privacy glass, cracking them up.

"How did you manage this?" he asked, sliding his hand down her waist and loving the feel of curves he knew he'd never get enough of.

"Oh, Hoyt and I worked it out to surprise you." She nestled closer and rested her head on his shoulder. "And I couldn't wait a minute longer to live here."

"Good, because I couldn't wait to have you here. Did you say goodbye to your parents?"

"With a promise we'd visit them in a few weeks."

He searched her face. "And?"

She nodded, her expression growing serious. "Yes, I told them about the nanny."

"Was it hard?"

"Worse for them, I think. Lots of tears and apologies." She shook her head. "I'm not looking into the past, Brock. I just want to look straight ahead, at the future. You know why?"

"Because we're spending it together."

"Yes." She leaned a little to her left and touched the button to open the window. A cool breeze blew in on his face as she tugged him closer to the bright light. "Look at that. What do you see?"

"Blue skies," he said, glancing out briefly before keeping his gaze on her.

"That's what's ahead for us," she said. "And when there's a storm…"

He took her face in his hands and kissed her forehead, holding his lips there as if he could imprint his love on her. "You won't be alone," he promised her.

"I'll be the opposite of lonely," she said on a laugh. "Which is…"

"Love." He pulled her closer and looked out at the blue skies of Boston and then at the woman he wanted forever in his arms. "The opposite of lonely is love."

Don't miss the next book in the

7 Brides for 7 Blackthornes
Multi-Author Series

LOGAN

by Samantha Chase

It's not easy being the youngest Blackthorne, and Logan has never shied away from a challenge. No matter what everyone thinks. Coming home to Maine finds him dealing with not only family surprises, but the shock of finding the caretaker's daughter all grown up.

Piper's dream is to design her own games, not play them. And Logan Blackthorne is the ultimate player. It's one thing to hang out with Logan as a friend, but he's far too charming for his own good.

Logan promises hours of pleasure, but should she settle for less than happily ever after?

Looking for more books by Roxanne St. Claire?

Check out www.roxannestclaire.com for a complete list
and buy links to her very popular series!

The Dogfather
Sit…Stay…Beg
New Leash on Life
Leader of the Pack
Santa Paws is Coming to Town
Bad to the Bone
Ruff Around the Edges
Double Dog Dare
Bark! The Herald Angels Sing
Old Dog New Tricks

The Dogmothers
Hot Under the Collar
(*and more coming soon!*)

Barefoot Bay
Secrets on the Sand
Seduction on the Sand
Scandal on the Sand

Barefoot in White
Barefoot in Lace
Barefoot in Pearls
Barefoot Bound
Barefoot with a Bodyguard
Barefoot with a Stranger
Barefoot with a Bad Boy
Barefoot Dreams
Barefoot at Sunset
Barefoot at Moonrise
Barefoot at Midnight

About the Author

Published since 2003, Roxanne St. Claire is a *New York Times* and *USA Today* bestselling author of more than fifty romance and suspense novels. She has written several popular series, including The Dogfather, Barefoot Bay, the Guardian Angelinos, and the Bullet Catchers.

In addition to being a ten-time nominee and one-time winner of the prestigious RITA™ Award for the best in romance writing, Roxanne has won the National Readers' Choice Award for best romantic suspense three times, as well as the Maggie, the Daphne du Maurier Award, the HOLT Medallion, Booksellers' Best, Book Buyers Best, the Award of Excellence, and many others.

She lives in Florida with her husband, and still attempts to run the lives of her young adult children. She loves dogs, books, chocolate, and wine, especially all at the same time.

www.roxannestclaire.com
www.twitter.com/roxannestclaire
www.facebook.com/roxannestclaire

SIGN UP FOR HER NEWSLETTER AND RECEIVE
A FREE FULL LENGTH NOVEL!
www.roxannestclaire.com/newsletter/